Corporal of the Mounted

★

BLACKIE & SON LIMITED
16/18 William IV Street,
Charing Cross, London, W.C.2
17 Stanhope Street, Glasgow

BLACKIE & SON (INDIA) LIMITED
103/5 Fort Street, Bombay

BLACKIE & SON (CANADA) LIMITED
Toronto

OAKFIELD   SUNDAY

SCHOOL

Presented to

Tommy   Arnott

for   excellent

attendance

G.J.G.103 Printed in England

F 649

" I'LL GIVE YOU JUST FIVE MINUTES "

Page 101

Frontispiece

CORPORAL
OF THE MOUNTED

*

L. Charles Douthwaite

WITH FRONTISPIECE BY R. ELVIS

BLACKIE & SON LIMITED
LONDON AND GLASGOW

To
Those Splendid Trail-Breakers
THE SNOWSHOE SQUAD
Royal Canadian Mounted Police
Past and Present

Printed in Great Britain by Blackie & Son, Ltd., Glasgow

CORPORAL OF THE MOUNTED

CHAPTER I

Corporal Steer follows the Trail

There was the pad of moccasined feet from the veranda outside, and the orderly room door opened. Leather-textured face concerned, Eli Fargus stood before the table where Corporal Larry Steer, in charge of the Royal Canadian Mounted Police detachment at Tamrack, Yukon territory, was busy with his monthly returns.

" What good wind's blown you along?" Larry demanded good-humouredly.

The storekeeper, however, shook his head.

" Not such a good wind," he said shortly. " An Indian's just come in to report that old Bill Neate's so sick that if he isn't in hospital pretty quick he's goin' to peg out."

One of his principal jobs being to look after the dwellers in remote places, Larry thrust his papers into a drawer.

" Then I guess I'd better pull right away,"
he said decisively, and the storekeeper registered
approval.

" Me bein', as you might say, the father of
this here community, I'd be glad to know how
he makes out," he responded.

Larry nodded. As the wealthiest man in the
township, the storekeeper liked to assume responsibility for those less fortunate than himself.

" I'll 'phone you as soon as I get back,"
Larry agreed, and half an hour later was mushing
his team down the straggling, snow-covered
street on his way to Jackfish. As he reached the
outskirts, however, he was hailed from one of
the wayside cabins.

Larry *woa-d* the team; turned to speak to
Louis Pierre Lefevre, the squat-framed, bright-
eyed French-Canadian trapper, with whom he
had formed a queer but lasting friendship.

" Where you 'eadin' for, anyway?"   Louis
Pierre demanded, with a glance at the closely-
packed sledge.

" Fetching in old Bill Neate," Larry explained.
" They tell me he's pretty sick."

Louis Pierre looked concerned.

" Then, believe me, I not delay you," he
said quickly. " I'll be glad if you'll let me know
when you pull in so I can go see 'im. A good
scout, that old one."

" I'll do just that," Larry promised, and forty-eight hours later, after one of the swiftest mushes of his experience, he *woa-d* his team outside Bill Neate's cabin, inside where he discovered that old-timer lying in the corner bunk.

" Couldn't've lasted a whole lot longer—not without help," he said weakly, and Larry agreed. Appendicitis was the trouble, as, due to an almost complete lack of vegetables, so often it was. And if the old warrior's life was to be saved, there was no time to be lost.

After a couple of hours rest for himself and the team, Larry laced his charge into a caribou robe for the journey. As he was on the point of helping him to the sledge, however, Neate jerked his head towards the opposite corner.

" Lift up that rug, do you mind," he said quietly, " and go bring up what I got packed away in the cellar there."

There were half a dozen steps down to the dug-out that, in those northern cabins, are used as a food store in warm weather. Here Larry's torch disclosed a score of the gold-bricks old Bill had " burnt " from high-grade quartz in a home-made furnace.

" As you suggest, I guess it'll be safer to take this along," he agreed, and packed the gold carefully in the sledge.

" Thanks a lot," Neate said appreciatively.

" As that's a good part of what I aim to retire on, I'd just hate to lose it."

" When do you expect to quit?" Larry demanded interestedly.

" Soon's I can sell the claim and book a passage to the Old Country," the old man replied decisively.

That return was a hard and anxious mush, and once they pulled into Tamrack it was with considerable relief that Larry saw his charge safely to hospital.

After that, he went to his friend Pierre, who greeted him with a grin that faded to concern at Larry's fatigue-ravaged face. Keeping a fire going for the sick man had cost him two night's sleep.

" Sit down while I get you eats," the French-Canadian said solicitously, and refused to talk until his friend had eaten, and their pipes were going.

" Doc. Pearson says that with a bit of luck he'll have old Bill on his feet again in a week or two —and without having to operate at that," Larry announced.

Pierre's leather-textured face brightened.

" Fine!" he exclaimed. " 'Is 'eart isn't too good, anyway, so that I doubt it would 'avé stood up to an operation. Soon, I go to the 'ospital to see 'ow 'e make out."

Actually, old Bill made a surprisingly good recovery, so that within a month of his admittance to hospital he was fit to return to his claim.

" It'll only be to pack what gear I need for the Old Country, anyway," he explained to Larry on the day of release.

" And to sell the claim," Larry reminded him. " With all that high-grade quartz, you should get a pretty good price."

The old man nodded.

" I'm not letting it go under twenty-five thousand dollars, anyway," he said definitely. " I'll call in an' say good bye as I pull out."

But to Larry's surprise, and to Pierre's, the old man left without a word—and the next thing Larry heard was that Eli Fargus had bought the claim, and installed his nephew, and only living relative, to work and manage it.

" If Eli gets any work out of Tom Wilson," Pierre remarked pessimistically, " 'e will be ver' lucky. A wall-propper and a bar support, that idle one."

Larry nodded.

" He sure does dream the hours away, all right," he agreed, and looked up sharply as the orderly room door crashed open, and a panting Indian came in.

" Charlie Woods he says for you to come to him right now," the Ojibway announced, and

hardly had the words left his mouth before
Larry was reaching for his boots and mackinaw.
His junior constable had left on patrol a few
days before, and would not have sent for him
hot-foot like this unless for something uncommonly serious.

" What might be the trouble?" Larry demanded, but the Ojibway shook his head.

" Charlie not say," he answered.

Travelling by forced stages, it was the evening
of three days later when Larry hit the edge of
the Reserve, where, in company with Chief
Starblanket, Woods was awaiting him.

" Come right along, and I'll show you," he
said soberly, in reply to Larry's question, and
making for the river that bounded the Reserve
a couple of miles away, followed its course down-
stream a farther few hundred yards to a point
that was known as Freshwater Creek. Here, he
stopped and pointed.

" Take a look at that," he said quietly.

But, his heartbeat suddenly quickened, Larry
had seen already. Caught in the high reeds of
the shallows was something grey-white and
ominous.

" As there was no danger of it shifting, I
decided to leave it where it is until you came
along," Woods supplemented.

Larry nodded; slipped off boots and breeches;

waded into the stream to make his examination.

In a half-hunched, half spreadeagled position, the body, that of a middle-aged or elderly man, Larry judged, was entirely naked. It was also entirely headless.

He took a long glance up-stream.

"Killed quite a distance from here," he pronounced confidently at last. "Pushed through a hole in the ice, and carried down by the current. . . . First thing we've to find is how long he's been dead."

They brought the body ashore and, placing it reverently on a hand toboggan, took it into Doctor Pearson at Tamrack.

"Been dead for about a month," he pronounced, after a first examination. "No indication of the cause of death. Tell you more, though, when I've made the post-mortem."

"Probably shot through the head," Larry suggested, adding: "And that head we've got to find if it takes a year."

When he went back to put the Reservation through a fine tooth-comb, one of the last of those he interviewed was Hungry Hail, a gaunt "free" Indian, who, having drifted into the Yukon from the Hudson Bay country only a few months before, had earned his keep by supplying the camp with kindling-wood.

"One moon and "—he thought for a moment

—" three suns since," he reported in Ojibway, " Hungry Hail was returning with a load from the woods. As the sun went down, Hungry Hail made camp in a clearing that was cut off from another and bigger clearing by a hedge of scrub.

" Though they could not see me because of this barrier, at the far side was a camp with two white men."

Larry nodded encouragement. Hungry Hail would tell his story in his own way, and would hate to be hurried.

" In the darkest of the night," the Indian went on slowly at last, " Hungry Hail was awakened by a sound."

" What kind of a sound?" Larry asked, as, this time a shade uncertainly, the Ojibway paused.

" Had it been louder, Hungry Hail would say it came from a gun," he said at last.

" You mean," Larry suggested quickly, " like a pistol would make if it was fixed under, say, a heap of blankets?"

Eagerly, for an Indian, the Ojibway nodded.

" Under a big heap of blankets," he qualified.

Here, then, was the first real clue. Further, the use of a silencer-equipped pistol went to show that, far from a killing in the heat of quarrel, this was a cold-blooded murder of premeditation.

" And then?" Larry questioned, suspecting there was more to come.

" Because he had worked hard and late, Hungry Hail sleep the next morning until the sun is high," the Ojibway supplemented gravely. " By then—of the two white men who had made camp across the clearing, but one remained."

" Did you see what became of the one who was left?" Larry asked, but the Indian shook his head.

" Hungry Hail pull out while the white man was there still," he said with finality.

Further questioning, moreover, elicited only that the Ojibway's sight of the survivor was so vague as to be useless, and that his description of the one who disappeared might have applied to nineteen men in twenty.

When the two policemen followed Hungry Hail to the old camp-site, it was not long before Larry's suspicion that this was the scene of the murder was confirmed, for intensive sifting of the camp-fire ashes disclosed metal trouser buttons and a belt buckle.

" All very interesting," Larry observed slowly during a few minutes rest, " but what we need is that missing head. And that I'm going to find if I have to put every inch of the area through a fine-mesh sieve."

Accordingly, Starblanket recruited a party from the Reserve, and for the next few days the search went on unceasingly, but for a long time without success.

It was Woods who made the discovery at last. After a strenuous morning, the two policemen met in a grass-grown clearing to compare notes over their midday meal.

Suddenly, a sandwich half-way to his mouth, Woods' gaze, that had been straying idly about him, became fixed.

" That's queer," he said slowly, and pointed.

Following the direction of his friend's finger, Larry's glance, too, remained stationary. The country was thick with snowshoe rabbits, with their burrows equally in evidence. But while most of these holes were circular and wide-mouthed, and with the excavated mould heaped promiscuously about the opening, the one Woods indicated was small and irregular, with the earth banked neatly and smoothly about it.

" Looks as if the original entrance had been filled in just after break-up, when the earth was soaked with melted snow," Woods said slowly. " Then, when the hot sun dried it out, it kind of crumbled away, leaving only that small hole."

" I think maybe you're right," Larry agreed, and got up to investigate.

He had no difficulty in enlarging the opening;

the earth came away almost to the touch, to disclose a hole considerably bigger than that normally made by a burrowing rabbit.

And when he thrust his arm down the opening, his fingers encountered something that was hard, and round, and smooth.

With a meaning glance at his opposite number, he produced his hunting-knife; dug away the earth so that his fingers could obtain the necessary hold.

When, eventually, his hand came away, he was holding, if not a human head, what was left of one. A skull, with a neatly-bored hole in the forehead, and the surface faintly blackened as if by fire.

Contemplating that grim relic, Larry pursed his lips.

" I'll bet a month's pay and allowances that this belongs to the body all right," he said confidently. Adding, less confidently. " But we're going to have one awful job to prove it."

" Better take it along to Doc. Pearson," Woods suggested. " There may be some way he can tell. Surprising what medical science can do these days, anyway."

Larry nodded.

" One of our big difficulties, of course, is that we haven't the foggiest idea who the murdered man is," he pointed out. " Not a local, anyway, because unless it's someone from one of the very remote cabins, there doesn't happen to be anyone missing."

" I'll say that's our big handicap, all right," Woods agreed unhesitatingly.

" And as we're not going to get anywhere until it's overcome," Larry said practically, " while I get back to Tamrack to see Doc. Pearson, I want you to ride round to every cabin in the area to find out, first if the owners are there still, and second, if any strangers were noticed on any day near the material dates."

" I'll do just that," Woods agreed.

It was almost on the outskirts of Tamrack that Larry noticed a figure trailing a hand-toboggan ahead, whom a closer view disclosed as Tom Wilson, Eli Fargus's nephew.

" Just pullin' into Tamrack for supplies," he explained, as Larry drew rein.

Mostly in bottles, it struck Larry with an unenthusiastic glance at the shambling, untended, figure. From the police point of view, of course, there was nothing really wrong with Tom; it was just that he was so bone idle that until he went on to old Bill Neate's claim, he had never done a decent day's work in his life.

" How's the claim making out?" Larry inquired curtly, and Tom's dull eyes lighted.

" A *pret*-ty good output, I'll tell the ring-tailed world," he said with every evidence of self-satisfaction. "Nearly sixty ounces last week, and the seam showin' no sign of peterin' out——"

"I'd buy a new mackinaw with some of the proceeds, if I were you," Larry suggested shortly, for the claim-holder was clad in a garment that, ragged and dirt-encrusted, would have been discarded by any hobo on the road.

Wilson's face registered protest.

"Then you'd be mighty clever," he sneered; "seein' that with the stage held up through flood, no supplies 've bin able to get through for weeks. There isn't a darn mackinaw on sale in the town."

That, Larry had to acknowledge, might be the case. Everything Tamrack wore, and most of what it ate, was brought in by caterpillar tractor from Dawson, and when the melted snow rushed down from the foothills in the spring, there were times when the low-lying trails were unnegotiable.

"If you like to call in at the barracks, I'll make you a present of one," he said curtly.

Wilson brightened.

"You mean that civvy one you used to wear —yeller cross-stripes over purple?" he asked eagerly.

Larry nodded. On the winter trail, bright colours are necessary for the eyes as a contrast to a landscape of unbroken snow, and that lately-discarded garment was a veritable Joseph's coat.

" Fine!" said Wilson enthusiastically. " I'll come with you right now."

From the barracks, after unearthing and handing over the discarded mackinaw, Larry made his way to the hospital, where he discovered Doc. Pearson—a little Scottish terrier of a man—who looked up alertly from his test-tubes as the policeman came in.

" Found that head yet?" he demanded sharply, coming at once to the point.

" We've found what's left of one, anyway, though only you can say for certain if it's the right one," Larry responded gravely, and, relating the circumstances of the discovery, handed that grim relic over.

For the moment, however, the doctor gave it only a superficial examination.

" Burnt in a fire that wasn't hot enough to consume the bone," he pronounced. " Probably that's why the murderer hid it where he did—to save time, and enable him to make his getaway from the scene of the killing. A pretty good hiding-place he chose, as well; but for the dry spell we've had lately, it might not have been discovered for years."

Larry nodded; all that had occurred to him already.

" Anything else?" he asked shortly.

Turning the skull slowly in his hands, the doctor's expression changed suddenly to an interest that was less professional than personal. Without speaking, he got up and went over to the cabinet in the corner, from where he took out a file and examined a record.

Returned to the bench, he made a further examination of one particular part of the skull through a powerful reading-glass. And when at last he replaced that grim relic on the bench, the face he turned to Larry was strained, and rather grey about the mouth.

" I can tell you who the murdered man was," he said shortly, and Larry felt his heart-beat quicken.

" Who?" he demanded shortly.

" Old Bill Neate," the doctor said decisively.

Knowing that Doc. Pearson was the last man to make an unsupported statement on such a serious subject, Larry succeeded in keeping a grip on himself. Further, in the few moments before he replied, he put in some intensive thought.

Though it was accepted that Neate had fulfilled his intention to leave for the Old Country, beyond his absence from the claim, what evidence was there that, actually, he had gone? Another thing that, however subconsciously, had always

stuck at the back of Larry's mind, was that the
old man had called to say good-bye neither to
himself nor anyone else.   And as Larry knew
Bill Neate, that was to the last degree unlike
him.

Suddenly another thought came.

" How can you tell?" he asked in a controlled
voice.

Doc. Pearson pointed a not too-steady finger
at a slight wedge-shaped depression in the skull,
just over where, in life, the left ear had been.

" I treated Bill for that injury," he said quietly.
" It was caused by an accident that happened to
him before you took over the detachment—his
axe-head flew off the handle when he was chop-
ping kindling.   And though I recognized the
wound at once, I said nothing until I was able
to confirm it by consulting my notes on the
case."

He paused, and then went on.

" Another thing.   When I made the post-
mortem on the body, there was evidence of
recent appendix trouble—just the same as old
Bill suffered from when you brought him into
hospital."

Larry made a mental calculation as to dates.

" I'll use your 'phone, if you don't mind," he
said, and in due time was connected with divisional headquarters at Dawson.   After twenty

minutes delay, the result of inquiries there came through.

Bill Neate had neither been seen about the town from where the stage left—nor had left for Whitehorse—that was the only route to England —on any of the relevant dates.

" Although, of course, I accept your identification," Larry pointed out to the Doctor, " knowing what juries are, I think we'd best have some corroboration. Anything you can suggest?"

Doc. Pearson nodded.

" Sure," he said confidently. " Go see your friend Pierre Lefevre. He took the case over from me when I was called away to Whitehorse; used to bandage Bill every day."

" Thanks a whole lot," Larry said gratefully, and made for the French-Canadian's cabin, which was to have been his next call in any case; he had come to rely quite a lot on the little *habitant's* shrewdness.

But as it happened, there was no interview.

The cabin was empty.

" You seekin' Louis Pierre Lefevre?" The stridently voiced query came from that notorious gossip, Mrs. Oddy, who lived in a cabin immediately across the way.

Larry admitted that he was.

" Went off hoss-ridin' with Eli Fargus close

on an hour ago. Seemed in a mighty hurry too," Mrs. Oddy shrilled, shoe-button eyes alive with curiosity as Larry crossed over to her.

" Which direction?" he demanded curtly, aware, quite illogically, of a sudden trepidation.

" Down the trail," she replied, with a sweep of her arm towards the open country. " I'll tell you somethin' else, as well," she added mysteriously.

" And that is?" Larry prompted, and the gossip sniffed aggressively.

" Seems kinder sought after, all of a sudden, that Frenchman does," she observed, eyeing Larry closely. " First Eli; third you."

" And what about Number Two?" Larry demanded quickly.

Mrs. Oddy shrugged ample shoulders.

" That roustabout, Tom Wilson," she said unpleasantly. " Came up all of a lather, and when I told him Pierre'd gone off with his uncle, asked where he could borrow a horse."

Larry was more disturbed still as he turned away.

Woods was using the only horse at the barracks, so leaving a note for him to follow at speed, Larry set off at once. With the trail so narrow and overgrown, he would travel as fast on foot as his quarry on horseback, anyway.

Stark fear at his heels, he did not make camp

until the moon was high, and in spite of a rain-
storm that lasted for a good half-hour, did not
awaken until the first flush of dawn. Twenty
minutes later, after a hurried breakfast of hard
biscuit and tea, he was on the move again.

It was in the middle of the morning when,
with a bitten-off exclamation, he pulled up
sharply in his stride. Until that moment he had
taken for granted that Eli was making directly
for Bill Neate's claim, but here the rain-softened
ground showed unmistakably that the horses
had turned from the main trail to one so newly-
made that only a woodsman of his own experience would have detected its existence. Indeed,
had it not been for those tell-tale hoof-marks,
Larry himself would have passed it by.

But where in Sam Hill, he asked himself
fearfully, was Eli making for? And for what
purpose?

With the answer that sprang ready-made to
his mind, his heart took a leapfrog bound to his
throat, and for a moment the landscape quivered
before his eyes like rocks in a heat-haze.

Tying a brightly coloured handkerchief to the
scrub as a sign to Wood, he set off on the new
line.

Overgrown and unbeaten as was the trail,
with that new and even more terrible fear jib-
bering at his heels, stopping neither for rest nor

food, he estimated his progress as a steady five miles an hour.

At last the trail widened and smoothed out, so that he suspected he was nearing its end. Then, at a sharp turn, it developed to a wedge-shaped clearing, tree-grown at the narrow end, and with a wood on the farther side.

Backed snugly against the pines, was a cabin, desolate-looking, as if it had been unlived in for a great length of time, though now there was a feather of smoke from the chimney. A cabin that, with so many hundred square miles to patrol, Larry had not known even to exist.

Moccasins silent on the leaf-mould, he pulled up sharply in his stride. A horse was tethered to a tree a hundred or so yards ahead.

Advancing purposefully across the open, was a figure whose upper portion was clad in a garment as familiar to Larry as it was brilliantly coloured.

While he stood for a moment, hesitating as to his own next move, the issue was taken terribly out of his hands. The cabin window crashed open; face distorted, and a rifle in his hand, Eli Fargus appeared. More quickly, almost, than the eye could follow, the rifle was levelled. A detonation; a sharp spearpoint of flame.

The advancing figure checked; hands gropingly outstretched, stumbled; following a couple of knee-bent, staggering paces, crumpled to ground, and there, face downward, lay.

One of Larry's best attributes as a policeman was his refusal either to panic or to act on impulse, and he did neither now. If he attempted to advance across the clearing, the odds were a hundred to one that he, too, would be shot, and in all probability Woods after him. Far better, then, to wait until either his opposite number showed up, or the fast advancing darkness afforded the necessary cover.

As Larry came to his decision, the cabin door opened, and Fargus came out; face unpleasantly alight, advanced to the dead man; turned the body over.

Never in his life had Larry seen so swift, or so awful, a change of expression as came into the murderer's face as his eyes fell on that dead man. One instant his countenance was all evil anticipation; the next, so convulsed with a mingling of horror and grief as almost to pass beyond the human.

Then, with a low, inarticulate cry, he threw up his hands, and staggered blindly back to the cabin.

There was the jingle of a bit, and turning, Larry saw Woods riding down the trail. In response to Larry's gesture demanding silence, his opposite number dismounted, hitched his horse to a tree; advancing, listened intently while Larry explained the position in detail.

" Now there's the two of us, and with Louis Pierre at his mercy, I'm not waiting for darkness or anything else," Larry said definitely, drawing his revolver from its holster as he spoke. " You wait here, see what comes to me—and then be guided by circumstances. But, whatever happens, remember you've to get Pierre out of that cabin alive."

Woods knew his man too well to argue; if for no other reason, as senior officer it was up to Larry to take the first risk.

" I'll do just that," the constable agreed quietly. " Good-luck, old-timer."

Nodding appreciation for the genuine solicitude of the tone, without another word, and expectant of a shot with every stride, Larry doubled across the clearing. To his surprise, no shot came, so that he pulled up immediately beneath the window.

He listened intently, but no sound came from within.

At last, revolver at the ready, he raised himself inch by inch to window-level—to discover himself looking straight at Fargus—and the muzzle of a rifle. And in the infinitesimal moment before his finger pressed the trigger of his revolver, and he ducked incontinently below window-level, Larry saw still another expression flash into the face behind the rifle-barrel—this time, one of undiluted *hate*.

To avoid any downward shot that might be forthcoming, he edged cautiously a few feet along the cabin wall. Again no shot came, nor any sound from within.

Following an interminable interval when nothing happened at all, a pebble fell close by, and, turning, Larry saw that Woods was gesturing that he would make for the farther side of the cabin, and having reached there, they should make their entrance simultaneously.

As no man can fire a rifle in two directions at once, and with the French-Canadian as the first consideration, Larry nodded his agreement.

The constable disappeared, and it was a tribute to his woodmanship that no further sound came until the low-pitched whistle from the farther side of the cabin. Whereupon Larry jerked to the upright, pushed the window back on its hinges, and swarmed through the opening.

Still again, and to his relief, the expected shot did not mature; nor, as Woods joined him from the opposite window, was there any sign of Fargus.

The living-room was small, roughly furnished, and with a door at either side. While Wood made for the one on the right, Larry turned the handle of the other—and, at what the opened door disclosed, was across that kitchen-outhouse in a single stride.

Because, there, bound tightly with caribou thong to a home-made chair, was Louis Pierre Lefevre—whose eyes fastened on Larry with a relief that was not all for his own rescue.

" And when I say I'm glad it's you," the *habitant* remarked fervently when Larry had untied the cords, " that's not the 'alf of it!"

Before Larry could reply, there was a shout from Woods—a cry with something in its quality that brought them to the other room at speed.

There, stretched full-length on the single bunk, a bullet through the base of the lung from that quick shot of Larry's, was Eli Fargus.

There was nothing to be done, for he was dead.

" Better Eli Fargus than Corporal Steer," the French-Canadian pointed out logically, when they were in the other room again. " Now I tell you I was afraid it was *you* who'd stopped that second shot."

" What I can't get at," Larry said, pulling himself together, " is why you didn't call for help."

Louis Pierre shrugged eloquently.

" Because Eli said if I did 'e would shoot me," he explained reasonably. " And by then, I—Pierre Lefevre—knew too much about that *cochon* to 'ave any doubt that 'e would do just that."

After a minute's pause for thought, Larry nodded agreement.

" In the position he was in, having murdered Bill Neate—it was his body we found in the river, incidentally—another killing would have made no difference, anyway. . . . But, what I can't understand, is why he brought you here at all, or why you agreed to come?"

This time the *habitant's* shrug was more eloquent, even, than before.

" 'E told me you'd been caught in a bear-trap," he explained, " and that as 'e knew I'd dressed a 'ead-wound of old Bill Neate's some time ago, maybe I'd be able to 'elp with the nursing. . . . Then, once we were inside the cabin 'ere, 'e—showed 'is 'and; told me about you finding the —the skull, 'ose it was, and that 'e wasn't leaving me in Tamrack to confirm Doc. Pearson's identification of it."

He hesitated.

" Me—I do not think—at the end, anyway —'e was quite sane," he added definitely.

" Sane enough to murder Bill Neate and swipe both his gold and his claim," Larry commented grimly.

To his surprise, however, Louis Pierre shook his head.

" It wasn't Eli 'oo killed Bill Neate," he said levelly, and Larry looked his astonishment.

" Who then?" he demanded breathlessly.

" The only person Eli love more than 'e love 'imself," the French-Canadian told him. " Tom Wilson, the son of 'is dead sister. When Tom call at the 'ospital, and saw all those gold bricks where the old man 'ad insisted they should be put under 'is own eye, and Bill told 'im he was pulling out for the Old Country the moment 'e could sell 'is claim, the opportunity—and the temptation—was too much for Tom. When Bill left 'ospital, Tom followed — and shot 'im over the camp-fire as 'e sleep—But you know the rest."

" Except how Eli came to connect Tom with the killing," Larry pointed out.

Louis Pierre shuddered slightly.

" There," he said, " you 'ave the 'ole tragic business. Banking on the old man's affection— knowing that the last thing Eli would do was give 'im away—Tom told 'im all about it."

Woods broke in then.

" But *why*, for the love of Mike?" he demanded, and Larry looked at him commiseratingly.

" Be your age, m'lad!" he said reprovingly. " How could a man who'd never earned a cent in his life buy a claim the owner had refused to sell for less than twenty-five thousand dollars?

(F 649)

As Louis Pierre here points out, to make his taking over the claim in any way plausible, he'd no *choice* but to tell."

For a long moment there was silence. Then Larry said, reflectively:

" I suppose it was just retribution—on both —that the end should have been that Eli was the direct cause of Tom's death."

Breath catching sharply in his throat, Louis Pierre regarded him wide-eyed.

" Eli kill Tom, do you mean?" he gasped, and Larry nodded.

" Sure," he confirmed soberly. " With that first shot you heard. Tom was wearing that old yellow-and-purple mackinaw I've just discarded —and Eli mistook him for me!"

CHAPTER II

Corporal Steer delays an Arrest

Larry Steer was crossing the parade ground on one of his periodical visits to headquarters, when he was hailed by Staff-Sergeant Wills.

" You've got to pull in Pete Ferris," he ordered, and the younger man whistled softly. Larry had always found Ferris decent enough. It was not more than a few months since the prospector had registered what was reported as the richest claim in years.

" What in Sam Hill's the charge?" he demanded.

" That at Goldeye, on June fifteenth, he did assault George Augustus Leckie, thereby occasioning actual bodily harm contrary to Section 295 of the Criminal Code," the sergeant replied solemnly. . . . " A pretty bad case, too, on the face of it. When Leckie came in to lay the complaint, he looked like he'd been struck by a cyclone; nose spread all over his map, and half his front teeth in his stomach."

Larry's eyes narrowed. Leckie, whom also

he knew, was not one of his favourites. Nor, in that neck-of-the-woods, was it customary for the loser in a free-for-all to come whining to the police.

" Do you mean Leckie trekked more than four hundred miles just to lay a complaint of being beaten up?" he said incredulously.

" *And* to swear out a warrant," the sergeant confirmed, handing over the document. " Pull out at noon to-day."

A week later Larry was leading his packhorse through the tree-belt that overlooked the Goldeye claim, when he heard axe-strokes. Following the sound, he found Peter Ferris cutting kindling. He was a spare but wiry man of early middle-age. At sight of the constable, his solid but anxious face lighted to welcome.

" What good wind's blown you hereabouts, Corp?" he inquired, advancing with outstretched hand.

Larry looked at him in some perplexity.

" For *you*, not such a good wind," he said, less officially than he felt was necessary. " Sorry, and all that, but you've got to come along." He advanced and touched his man on the shoulder as demanded by regulations. " I arrest you on a charge of assaulting George Leckie."

Dropping the looped tree-branch he was holding, Ferris stared at him. There was stark fear in his eyes, that in view of the comparative triviality of the charge, Larry found rather startling.

" But—but it was a fair scrap——", he stammered, and pointed to a still discoloured eye. His face turned savage.   " Besides, he said things about my Ellie I wouldn't take from no man."

Probably a more or less accurate account of what had happened, it occurred to Larry. Nevertheless, his orders were definite.

" Tell that to the magistrate," he said, not without sympathy.

In that harsh climate a claim could be worked only so many weeks in the year, and because of the long journey involved, the charge would take quite a time to clear. Ferris's face was dismayed, as he shouted:

" But I can't come! Not now, anyway!" His hand reached out to clasp Larry's shoulder. " Listen, Corp., put me on parole for two—three weeks. I'll come in, all right—the first minute I'm able. But with my Ellie as she is now, *I can't!*"

Here was a challenge that, in the ordinary way, Larry would have leapt in to answer. Now he only looked his man hard in the eyes.

" What's the matter with your wife?" he said quietly.

Ferris's muscles, that an instant before had been braced for conflict, relaxed.

" She's sick," he said unhappily. " And has been, for quite a while. Internal pains that fairly double her up. Doc. Harding, of Pickeral Landing, an' the only one in more'n a hundred miles, is away to the States; an' with not even an Ojibway woman within reach, there's only me to tend her." He seemed to droop. " An' what good's a man in a case like this ?"

As, in the more isolated parts of the north, the functions of the Mounted Police comprise anything between parson and postman, sanitary inspector and sexton, even this situation was not unprecedented.

" Forget I am one," Larry said, with more confidence than he felt. " Also—what won't be too easy—persuade your wife to do so as well. I may not hold a whole sheaf of certificates, but I passed my first two examinations as a doctor, and I'd've got through the final as well except that when my father was killed in a motor accident I pulled out from the Old Country so's my mother should have what little money there was."

As the two men crossed the clearing, a cry came out to them, bitten-off but pain-ridden, and at the sound Ferris broke into a run.

When, in turn, Larry passed through into the

rough but comfortably furnished room, the claim-holder was leaning over the spruce-and-chicken-wire bunk in the corner, with his fingers closed tightly about the hand of his wife.

She was a pretty little woman, though now her features were drawn with suffering. Nevertheless, she contrived a glance at Larry that was a mixture of welcome and inquiry.

" Listen, Mrs. Ferris," he said practically. " This kind of thing's a new one on your husband, and small wonder either, but as I'm more than half a doctor anyway, and have had quite a bit of experience among the Indians, you've just got to forget this "—he touched the buffalo-head on his mackinaw collar that was his badge of office—" and tell yourself I'm the family physician."

The indignation that flashed into her eyes for a moment was replaced by long-founded fear, and that, in turn, gave way to something of appreciation.

It did not take long for Larry to diagnose the case as one of acute appendicitis. He knew, further, that if her life was to be saved he would have to operate, and at once. And though, actually, he had never performed the operation himself, he had seen it done so often in his student days that, unless there were complications, he thought he would be able to manage.

" You can tell Peter what to do, I guess, anyway," the patient said faintly, when this was explained, and after that there was no more difficulty. Fortunately, there was a case of instruments in Larry's pack, that he carried in case of emergency, together with a bottle of chloroform.

In the next tense half-hour or so, Ferris's solicitude was so feverish that he was of little help. Nevertheless, the moment came when Larry was able to hand him the instruments to clean while he himself settled the patient more comfortably.

For one apparently so frail, Mrs. Ferris made a good recovery, and in that time of convalescence Larry's liking for his hosts matured. They were honest, hard-working, and essentially kindly.

So one day he left his patient in charge of her husband and set out for the Leckie claim. As this was the only trail in the district that did not run either through scrub or woodland, he covered the half-dozen miles in not much over the hour.

Arrived there, he was not impressed with what he saw. There was no one on the workings; development was sketchy, and the excavated quartz untidily piled. The only evidence of expert workmanship, indeed, was in the clay furnace that had been erected some little distance from the trench, and even this had not been used.

Inside the cabin, that was as neglected as the workings, he discovered Leckie, a flabbily-built man with closely-set, light-blue eyes, busily making a toboggan. He looked a little startled at Larry's appearance, but, greeting him boisterously, waved a hand to indicate his work.

" Gettin' good and ready for freeze-up," he explained. " My old toboggan was only small, so I'm makin' somethin' better. . . . Anythin' I can do for you, or did you just call in when passin'?"

As was his custom, Larry went straight to the point.

" Now that the dust of conflict's subsided, as you might say," he suggested, " what about withdrawing that warrant you swore against Pete Ferris?"

Leckie shook his head.

" Sorry, an' all that," he said definitely, " but there's nothin' doin'."

Larry attempted persuasion.

" Hasn't anyone told you his wife's a mighty sick woman?" he protested. " Surely you don't aim that she shall be left alone while we make the trip to headquarters?"

Leckie's expression was unpleasant.

" A feller with all that highgrade's no cause

to beat up a feller that hasn't got nothin'," he said, and paused, shooting a quick glance at Larry. " How's his missis makin' out, anyway?"

The corporal's eyes narrowed. To refuse clemency, and inquire after the victim in one and the same breath, was not so good!

" Sits up for a little in the daytime, but has to turn in good and early," he said shortly. " And after the things you said that led to Pete beating you up, if you were any kind of a man you'd be good and glad to have him look after her."

Leckie sneered.

" I'm all the kinds of man I need to be," he said, " so I guess we'll let it go at that. . . ." He hesitated. " What day do you pull out with your prisoner?"

" What's that to do with you, anyway?" Larry demanded uncordially.

" I gotter be there to testify, ain't I?" Leckie protested loudly.

Larry turned to the door.

" We'll start on the morning of the day after to-morrow," he said curtly, and left.

He put in a spell of pretty hard thinking on the homeward trail—there were elements in the situation that struck him both as peculiar and needing explanation. . . .

Back at the Goldeye claim, he found Ferris engaged in a careful extraction of the narrow, rust-coloured seam that threaded an uncertain way through the darker, less productive quartz.

" Soon's freeze-up comes I aim to ' bake ' this little lot," the prospector explained, indicating the result of his morning's work.

Larry nodded understandingly. Burnt in a furnace similar to Leckie's, the highgrade would yield all but a minute fraction of its gold. Judging from the pin-points of yellow that gleamed from the half-dozen or so samples he picked up to examine, that result would be considerable.

" How much does it run?" he inquired.

" From eight to twelve hundred dollars to the ton," Ferris said promptly, and Larry whistled.

" Where do you store it?" he asked, and Ferris waved his hand in the direction of a shed that stood midway between the claim and the cabin.

" In that there dog-stable," he said. . . .

It was not a cheerful farewell in which Larry took part two mornings later.

" Don't you worry, Mrs. Ferris," he reassured the tearful woman. " You'll have old Pete back with you before you know he's gone."

A pace that was brisk enough at the beginning, slowed down as the morning progressed. After the midday grub, indeed, Larry remained so long lounging over the fire that Ferris protested.

"Listen!" he burst out irritably. "This may be a picnic for you, but it's plain purgatory for me. You gotta remember that the sooner we reach headquarters, the sooner I'll be headin' for home—and Ellie!"

"You're going home right now," Larry said quietly, and told his astonished prisoner why.

It was dark when—the packhorse tethered a good mile away—they came within sight of the unlighted cabin. Soft-footed, they skirted the building; like shadows took station within sight of the dog-stable.

An hour passed; two; three; and all that broke the silence of a night when the stars were low and bright as hanging lamps was the occasional mournful cry of a loon.

Then, suddenly, the prisoner's fingers closed hard about Larry's arm. But already the corporal had seen the blur that, topping the rise, merged into the shadows as the trail descended.

Ten more minutes passed, and they heard nothing. Then the figure reappeared, distinct now, and toiling, yet with no accompanying sound.

Gradually he came still nearer; and, as Larry had expected, was seen to be trailing a toboggan, that, as he reached the dog-shed, he swung round to face the direction from where he had come.

Then he unscrewed the staple of the padlock, and passed inside.

There was the flash of a torch, a brief interval, and when the figure reappeared he was dragging a sack that he loaded on the toboggan. Swiftly, in the same silence, he loaded four or five others. At last he slipped into the traces and made for the homeward trail.

"Not a *bit* like it, Leckie!" Larry called equably, stepping into the open. Then he put Leckie under arrest. . . .

"A clever enough scheme, all right—if only he'd got away with it," Larry remarked to the staff-sergeant, when, with the charge-sheet duly signed, Leckie was safely in the cells.

"Tell me it again," Wills said interestedly.

"At a time when it was pretty obvious it was only a matter of days before Mrs. Ferris would be out of action—you must remember she was in pain pretty well all the time—Leckie handed Pete Ferris the insult he knew would make him lash out," Larry explained. "Then, all that was necessary to leave him free to raid the high-grade, 'burn' the gold, and be over the Alaskan border, was to swear out a warrant for Pete's arrest."

The staff-sergeant nodded.

"I know that part; but what was it put you wise?" he asked, and Larry grinned.

" The fact that, with only a low-grade claim, Leckie had built a furnace for burning high-grade," he explained. " And in a densely-wooded country, that he was making a toboggan so big that the only trail he'd be able to use it on was the one to—Ferris's claim."

CHAPTER III

Corporal Steer lays a Ghost

Larry Steer made no bones about getting rid of a caller in whom he had so little interest. Having made no attempt to adapt himself to the harder conditions of the north, already Charlie Bates, that persistently work-shy mendicant from the prairie provinces, had " borrowed " more dollars from him than it had been convenient to part with.

" If you need money, go out and cut wood," the policeman said curtly, the prevailing fuel shortage in mind. " There'll be plenty glad to give you eight or ten dollars a cord for it, anyway."

Sneering, Bates made for the door.

" With any luck, I'll be usin' ten-dollar bills for cigarette lighters before so very long," he said, and so confidently as to leave Larry wondering, though at the moment he had something more urgent on his mind.

Just when he had been promoted for bringing order to one of the toughest detachments in the Yukon, it had begun to look as if the Indians were out for trouble. And at all costs that had to be avoided.

" Those Ojibways," " Old Man " Rivers, the divisional superintendent had instructed him over the telephone a few days before his promotion, " have been on Three Lake Reserve for thirty odd years without trouble, and that's what it's up to you to see they go on doing."

Until a month or so ago, nothing could have been easier. Pot-a-Pie, the flattened-face chief, had always met him at the outskirts of the camp, escorted him to his own tepee, served him regally with moose-meat stew, cadged as much stick tobacco as his visitor could be induced to unload, put up the usual kick at the meagreness of Treaty Money, and parted an hour or so later with the customary Sign of Friendship.

Then came a day when Pot-a-Pie had not been there to greet him. Further, instead of the tribe forcing themselves on Larry's attention with the curt nods and laconic grunts that is the Ojibway idea of welcome, there were so few of the tribe within sight that it was like leading his horse through a semi-derelict camp.

Seated cross-legged and motionless at his tepee entrance, moreover, Pot-a-Pie's response to Larry's greeting had been both silent and sullen, and with an Indian in general and an Ojibway in particular, that is an ominous sign.

When the moment came for parting, and it was without the Sign of Friendship, it was more disturbing still.

That was a fortnight ago, and the reports that had come in meantime were not encouraging. So that, though normally his next visit was not due for a further couple of weeks, the corporal decided to load the packhorse and set off right away.

Arrived at the reserve, again there was no chief to greet him. There was, moreover, hardly a soul in sight, and with the queer, unnatural silence that prevailed, the corporal's heart sank. Unless he misread the signs, what was the matter with the camp was the most dangerous element of all with which he could be called upon to cope.

Fear!

Squatting alone in the far interior of his tepee, Pot-a-Pie looked up as his visitor appeared at the entrance. Only, without speaking, to lower his eyes again.

The corporal passed purposefully into the tepee, squatted immediately before the chief, filled his pipe from a bulging pouch, expelled a cloud of smoke, and passed the pouch to Pot-a-Pie.

He, after a momentary wrestle with temptation, shook a sullen head.

Watching the chief closely, Larry saw that the high-cheek-boned face was fallen away, and a little grey about the mouth. And at the back of the deeply-set eyes was suppressed but very active terror.

"What might happen to be the trouble, Chief?" Larry asked quietly.

The silence, sullen and brooding, lasted for so long that for a moment Larry wondered if any reply was to be forthcoming. At last, however, Pot-a-Pie spat aggressively in the dust of the floor.

"Thirty years and more has the Ojibway been on this reserve," he said in his own tongue, that Larry had made a point of learning. "Living peacefully, harming none, obeying a law he had no hand in making. Yet it seems that we must go," he added, a note in his voice it did the corporal no good to hear.

"I don't get you, Chief," he protested. "The reserve is yours; your home; given over to you by the Government for all time, and to which none but your people have any shadow of claim. Tell me who says otherwise, and, believe me, I'll deal with 'em."

The fear in his eyes even more evident than before, the Indian's thin-lipped mouth drew downward.

"In two words, Pot-a-Pie tell what you, the

Fork-Tongued One, know already," he said curtly.
" The Government."

Unpredictable as is the Indian mind, to the
corporal this came like a blow between the
eyes.

" By ' Government ', do you mean the Mounted
Police?" he demanded.

Shrugging gaunt shoulders, Pot-a-Pie spat
again.

" Are not the Yellerlegs the paid servants of
Government?" he demanded unpleasantly.

His face stern, the corporal shook his head.

" Governments come, and Governments go,
in turn to be replaced by others. But because
they are the servants only of the Great White
Chief Across the Water, the Red Coats remain,
unchanged and unchangeable—true friends of
their Indian brothers," he corrected, employing
the old respected name for the Force in deli-
berate contrast with the other's term of disparagement.

" Then why," demanded Pot-a-Pie hotly, his
eyes flaming, " do you let them send *Windigo*
to our camp, so that at last we must flee in terror
—while we are still alive?"

Momentarily, the corporal's breath caught.
Of all bad medicine, this was the worst he could
have been up against.

Windigo, the half spirit, half human, devil

of the north, ruthless, malignant, existing on the flesh of those he surprises asleep beside a burnt-out fire, is the most impregnable of all Indian superstitions, and the one most to be dreaded.

Haltingly, however, as if the very fact of narration went to accentuate the danger, the story came out.

Kept at bay only by the fires outside the tepees, each night in those last few weeks, *Windigo*, tall, hairy, flame-encompassed, and with a cry " louder than a hungry wolf ", had been hovering at the outskirts of the camp, so that the tribe was rapidly getting out of hand. It was only typical of the involved thought-process of the Indian that the visitation—if visitation, actually, it was—should be attributed to the machinations of an always mistrusted government.

Though not too successfully, the corporal probed as deeply as he considered expedient, but fear had bitten too deeply for reassurance. Finally, he looked the chief directly between the eyes.

" Even though you have called me the Fork-Tongued One, have I ever given you any but the true word?" he demanded levelly.

The chief returned the glance; then lowered his eyes.

" Pot-a-Pie spoke in haste," he admitted shamefacedly.

This was good hearing, and the corporal held out a hand that, after only momentary hesitation, the other took.

"Here, again, is the true word," the policeman said gravely. "Within the space of seven sunsets, I, Constable Steer of the Red Coats, will deal with *Windigo*, so that he will go, leaving you for ever in peace. . . . Can you hold the tribe until then?"

So far as is possible with an Indian, Pot-a-Pie flushed.

"Am I not Chief of the Ojibways?" he said with something of the old arrogance. And there, for the moment, the corporal was obliged to leave it.

On his way back to Tamrack to make his report, with his long experience of a country where so often a man's life may depend on a minute-to-minute vigilance, Larry kept a wary eye open. He had an idea that it was not only the Ojibways who were in danger.

As happens at intervals, the berry crop, upon which the bears feed immediately before hibernation, had failed on the foothills. When, to make up the shortage, the animals had come down to the river for fish, it was to find that already the salmon had left for the spawning grounds. Now, too hungry to take to winter quarters, the bears were roaming by and large in search of food. And though, full-fed, a bear is harmless enough, famished he is a very formidable proposition indeed.

Once, the mare plunging and trembling at the intimidating scent, he heard the crashing of tinder-dry branches that spoke of those marauders only a little way to the right of the trail. At another time, at the edge of a clearing, he caught a glimpse of a cinnamon bear who, at sight of him, fangs exposed, began ominously to advance, so that Larry had to shoot. . . .

. . . .

In the first of the swiftly-falling dark, the corporal took cover within measurable distance of Pot-a-Pie's tepee, that he judged would be the focal-point of whatever was to come.

Even with the western sky still floodlit with the ephemeral violet and daffodil of afterglow, the camp was fire-spangled, and as night closed down, the flames shone with ever-increasing clarity against the murk.

For a while, with all else black and formless about him, those fires, with the dim figures passing vaguely and uneasily before and beyond, was all he was able to distinguish.

Then, as the moon swung above the hill-tops, the landscape became more sharply defined, the trees silhouetted sharply against the horizon's purple-grey.

What sounds had come from an unnaturally subdued camp died at last, so that the silence was broken only by the laughter hoot of the owl, the thwack of a beaver's tail on the surface of the nearby lake, or the snapping bark of an otter.

The fires, however, remained; so many, and so constantly replenished, as to throw their surroundings into greater obscurity.   It was upon Pot-a-Pie's tepee, and the bush immediately overlooking it, that the corporal's stretched attention was directed.

Though the chief's fire dimmed, the figure squatting nearby remained motionless, and the embers unreplenished.   Exhausted by so many successive nights of vigil, Pot-a-Pie slept, so that at last his fire went out altogether.

More alert, now, than ever, the corporal's eyes travelled to the scrub; narrowed as his heart began to beat more quickly.

The figure which rose from the bush was tall and formless; glowing, as if from some inner, unearthly, light. To one less sceptical than the watcher, the phenomenon would have been terror-inspiring indeed. Certainly those within the camp found it so, for from every quarter came the fear-stricken wailing of women.

In the woods, it is not the loud noise that means danger, so that, while the stealthiest sound will jerk the sleeper to alertness, he will remain undisturbed through tumult. So it was that as the unearthly figure advanced, Pot-a-Pie did not stir.

The corporal, however, did—quickly, and with the silence of his own perfected woodsmanship. And as, one by one, the women dived for their tepees, the camp was stilled with the expectant hush of fear.

Quickly as he moved, moreover, it came to the corporal that, in his anxiety to escape observation, he had allowed his quarry too great a start, so there was danger that the intruder would reach the chief unmolested. And in the hand of that intruder was the glimmer of steel.

It was when the figure was within a score yards of the dead fire that suddenly the situation changed. From the farther side of a nearby tepee emerged the biggest cinnamon bear the corporal had ever seen.

Windigo, too, saw it — but too late. As, yelling, he turned to run, the bear was on him. . . .

Shouting to distract the beast's attention, the corporal dashed forward, unloosening the catch of his holster as he ran. Rising to the upright, and leaving his victim, the bear began slowly to advance, head rolling, spinal hair bristling.

Half a dozen paces away, the corporal checked, took a steady pull on himself. He saw, with relief, that the rising paw exposed the point below the shoulder-blade that, excepting for the eye, is the most vulnerable of all.

Three times the corporal fired, and the heavy .45 bullets crashed home. The bear roared, choked, fell—and lay still.

By this, Pot-a-Pie, aroused by the tumult, was bending over the motionless, and now only patchily luminous *Windigo*. Above the phosphorus-impregnated, roughly contrived, bearskin that was his disguise, stared the blood-streaked face of Charlie Bates. . . .

They carried him to Pot-a-Pie's tepee, where, after improvised first aid, he recovered a precarious consciousness.

" Guess I'm through," he muttered faintly. " But I was on a winner, all right, if I could've scared this bunch offen the reserve. Then, with the area thrown open, I could've registered my claim."

The corporal regarded him distastefully.

" Your claim to what?" he inquired.

" Feel in my pants pocket—and you'll find the richest specimens of highgrade quartz ever you set eyes on," Bates returned. " Chipped 'em from the rock in that clearin' a quarter mile east of Elbow Creek."

This time, with the Ojibway reassured, and his own problem solved, the corporal's look

was one more of compassion than of anger.
Nevertheless, groping in the injured man's pocket,
he produced a handful of grey-green quartz,
each specimen gleaming with pin-points of
yellow.

" You know your own business best, of course,"
he said tolerantly, " but, to me, this seems pretty
poor stuff to risk the rope for."

Startled, Bates' eyes travelled in turn from the
corporal's face to the specimens in his hand.

" What, for all that gold!" he protested.

The corporal shrugged; pitched the worthless
quartz, that is the novice's usual mistake, through
the tepee entrance.

" Even a ' desert rat ' like you should know
the difference between gold and iron pyrites,"
he pointed out.

CHAPTER IV

Corporal Steer encounters a Derelict

If Abner Pryde had saved even a small percentage of the money he had made in his years of prospecting, he would have been able to rent something better than the two-room suite over Charley Fisher's Lucky Strike Store at Tamrack.

But like so many of the old-timers, once Abner had developed a claim to production, back to his feet would come the itch for distant fields, and after that it was only a matter of time before the financiers owned the claim, and the saloon keepers all the purchase price but a grubstake for the next trip " out ".

Until, that is, he met Sadie O'Dowd, the school-teacher, whom he married out of hand, and in that understanding care the itching feet cooled and liquor lost its urge.

But as if Sadie was fortune enough to go on with, from that time forward Abner could do nothing right. Nor did the arrival of Abner Junior contribute to help already precarious finances.

Break-up was late that year, so that the season would be correspondingly short, and when Abner called in at the store, Charley Fisher was curter, even, than usual.

"Two months behind with the rent, and you've the gall to ask me to grubstake you," protested that disillusioned financier of optimism. "Why, by the time you're back, you'll owe more'n two hundred for rent alone. *And* you'll have all the winter to get through."

In view of the nights he had lain awake pounding at just these figures, this was telling Abner. So, even though the remedy would mean no time at all with Sadie and Junior, there was nothing else for it.

"Listen, Charley," he conceded desperately. "If I don't make a stake, I'll go trappin' soon's I pull in, and pay you that way. That's a promise."

A moment for consideration, and, however dubiously, Fisher nodded. Abner was a good old plug, and would stand by his word, anyway.

"I guess that'll have to go," he said resignedly. "So I'll stake you to seventy-five bucks, an' Sadie c'n have credit up to six dollars a week."

Abner released long-withheld breath, for without this last he could not have pulled out.

"You're a prince, Charley!" he said appreciatively, and after he had assembled his supplies, spent the remainder of the day patching a long-outworn canoe. . . .

The sun was swinging above the Indian reserve across the river when, after a restrainedly cheerful good-bye to Sadie, and a less untearful one from Junior, Abner embarked on the broad Saskatchewan next morning. Shoulders swaying easily to the stroke, and stopping for grub only at long intervals, he had covered a good seventy miles by the time he made camp.

Days of steady paddling through a chain of island-dotted lakes, and he cached the canoe and a proportion of the grub, and, load high on his shoulders, and tumpline wide across his fore-head, struck inland through the woods.

Then began a trek that not one prospector in fifty would have dared to risk. The trees were so thickly-growing as to shut out any sight of the lake fifty yards from the beach; overhead, the branches so interlaced as entirely to obliterate the sun that to nine out of ten was the only guide.

Well, the real woodsman should be independent of sun, stars, or compass. Didn't the crests of the pines point invariably to the north-east? Wasn't the bark thicker and the rings closer together on the northern side of a tree? And moose tracks mostly in places with a southern exposure?

What more did an honest-to-goodness woodsman need, anyway, except a memory for every turn of the trail, a good eye for the country ahead, and to remember to correct the human tendency to bear always left or right?

As he progressed, the ground-formation became more promising. No granite; just plain quartz, and that was all to the good. Once or twice, too, when he stopped to pan a specimen, he found " colour ". Not enough to count, but each time a little better than the last.

Except that here and there a barrier of windfalls forced a détour, and that only where muskeg thinned the trees was there any sight of the sun, the going was not too bad. But he sure was sick to the stomach of the sourbelly pork that, except for beans, flour, tea, and sugar, was all his meagre grubstake had been able to provide.

A good country for trapping, as well—he had never seen so much evidence of fur—tracks everywhere, from the hop-hop-and-slide of the otter, the miniature lion-paw impression of the lynx, the delicately-paired prints of the ermine, to the one-behind-the-other pad of the fox. He determined that if bad luck forced him out of Tamrack for the winter, this was where he would lay his trapline.

And plenty of game as well—moose, caribou, and deer—and to most this would have meant a

feast. But for the second of the two reasons why
he hated the thought of a winter on the traplines,
Abner was content to stick to his sourbelly. In
the war of twenty years ago the dimming of so
many human eyes had left him with an ineradicable
distaste for the sight; so that, ever since, he had
refused to take any life he was able to spare. In
these woods a man was only an intruder, anyway. . . .

It was in an area where the quartz gave a
richer " colour " with every mile, that, coming
towards him from the end of a natural drive
between the trees, he caught sight of what,
because of the awkward, hunched-up gait, he
mistook at first for a half-grown black bear.

Then, halted, and watching intently, his eyes
narrowed. Suddenly, with a bitten-off exclamation, he darted forward.

Only, with every pounding step, to become
more convinced that it was his second impression
that was correct.

Lurching vaguely-purposefully forward, the
creature did not see him until they were sepa-
rated only by a few yards. Then, glancing up,
he swung swiftly round, and with a sound midway between a gulp and a cry, made a shuffling
attempt to retreat between the trees.

Abner followed; in a few quick strides caught
up. As, croaking and mouthing, the creature

stopped, bending his arms about the emaciated body, Abner raised him from hands and knees to the upright.

Bone-thin from starvation, the man was as nearly naked as made no matter. Where the face was not grey with massed mosquitoes, it was so swollen as almost to overlay the sunken, red-shot eyes; the newly-grown beard alive with flies attracted by blood from the lacerated lips. Except that he was of middle age, and probably city bred, there was no indication of who or what he was, or of how long he had been in the woods.

Abner had been making for one of the grass-grown clearings that fringed the pools that, here and there, were formed by tributary streams from the distant lakes. He carried his by-now unconscious burden there, and laid him on outspread blankets.

It is certain that none but either a doctor or a woodsman could have pulled that derelict through; only later, when he came to learn the distance the lost man had wandered, was Abner able to realize the miracle of his survival.

Even after he was cleansed, and his wounds salved from the meagrely-equipped first-aid box; palms, knees and toes lacerated to the bone, still imbecile from starvation, shock, and exposure, he could give no account of himself.

Food was a difficult problem, as well; a starved man couldn't be fed on sourbelly. So, feeling like one who betrays a city, Abner snared snow-shoe rabbits for broth, and after that alternated these with the partridges that, having nothing but his rifle, he shot sitting.

There was no question of moving; it would be days even before the man was able to lift his head from the blankets.

Not that that mattered; with hospital the only place for his find, any chance of making a stake had gone already. It would be a winter on the trapline for Abner, all right.

Well—no use in whining; he'd been up against it too many times himself to quarrel with the Law of the Woods that, come what may, no help must be denied to those in need. . . . But he wasn't looking forward to the look in Sadie's eyes when he came to tell her he was leaving for the traplines straight away.

Even when " Crusoe " began to respond to treatment, he just lay on his blankets staring at the sky, every now and then breaking into the high-pitched, incoherent babble that ate into Abner's usually steel-wire nerves like acid into metal.

Gradually, however, these ravings came less often, with the patient able to sit up; later, to stand on his own feet; later still, and though as dependent on Abner as an ailing child on his mother, to walk.

By the time his charge was strong enough for the trek to the canoe, Abner knew they would be lucky to make the grade before freeze-up. Already the Crimson and Brown Youth, as the Ojibways call the Indian summer, had flamed the maples to scarlet; the woods at night filled with the crackling of tiny feet over leaves crisped by the hunting winds of autumn: louder, but less often, the sharp crack of a tree-branch torn from the trunk to line the winter home of some hibernating bear; the pool surface dotted with flotillas of waterfowl mobilized for winter migration; the high hay of the beaver meadows and river-grass burnished by the cold fire of the setting sun.

Beginning with a day that, bringing home what these woods had done to him, wrought Crusoe to almost unmanageable fear, it was a fortnight before they reached the lake. By then, however, except that his memory was non-existent, his brain was beginning to function.

It was late afternoon when they retrieved the canoe, but Abner neither waited for morning to set off, nor made camp until a couple of hours after dark. When they awakened next morning, with the sun a crimson disc against the grey backcloth of sky, the river edge was rimed with ice. . . .

With no spare clothing, and only a couple of blankets, it was so cold out there in the open, that waking, Abner added his own blankets to that of the shivering Crusoe, and after that insisted on him keeping them for the daytime as well. . . .

The ice forming more rapidly than it could be broken, so that there was no time to land and make a fire, the rest of that return trip was agony. . . .

There were no lights either from Tamrack or the Indian Reserve as Abner drew to the ice edge.

" Stay put," he ordered curtly, and swarmed out of the canoe with the expertness of long practice.

The ice cracked, but held. To distribute the weight, he edged the craft farther along.

" Now get ashore—lyin' flat, same as I did," he instructed with a wary eye on the manœuvre. " Work yourself along for twenty yards before you get to your feet. After that, make flat-out for the shore. . . ."

Abner, hauling the now unencumbered canoe after him, dragged it toboggan-fashion to the beach, so that all he had to do was get Crusoe to hospital. After that, to rake Sadie out of sleep to tell her that as they wouldn't have money for winter, he'd have to get his traps together straight away, and he'd rather have faced a cage of jaguars than that. It wasn't what she'd say that was going to hurt, but how she wouldn't be able to help looking.

However!

"Come right along," he said shortly, and guided his docile charge up the beach, and to the high boardwalk of the single, straggling, street, over where, by now, the night was fading to morning.

Wearing the mackinaw, coonskin cap, and spurred calf-high boots that is the Royal Canadian Mounted Police winter dress, a figure stepped out from the shadow of the Hudson's Bay Store.

"Who've we here, anyway?" a familiarly-deep voice demanded, halting them.

"Abner Pryde, me," that exhausted wanderer replied, not too amiably. "As for my side-kick here, you can search me, because I can't tell you."

A torch-beam flashed into the stranger's face, and there, for a matter of seconds, remained.

"But I can tell *you*!" Larry Steer said in a tone that jerked Abner's sleep-starved brain to alertness. "For the love of Mike, where did you find him?"

"In the woods around Herb Lake," Abner explained. "Bush crazy, and so near dead it was quite a while before he could travel. Who is he, anyway?"

" Andrew Merrilees, President of the Hearth and Home Tobacco Trust of New York. Hired Jake Molloy as guide on a fishing-trip—and Jake was found dead of heart-failure a month later beside a burnt-out camp-fire," Larry said informatively.

Hands closed hard about Abner's arm; the eyes that stared into his were newly rational.

" That's right!" " Crusoe " shouted tensely. " Andrew Merrilees, me!"

" Important feller, eh?" Abner suggested interestedly, as they made for the hospital, and the Mounted Policeman laughed shortly.

" If not, what do you think's drained this burg of men to make up search-parties?" he asked.

" Common humanity," Abner said promptly, and the constable nodded.

" Sure," he agreed. Adding:

" *And* the reward of twenty-five thousand dollars for whoever found and brought him in alive."

CHAPTER V

Corporal Steer deals in Counterfeit

The door of the log-built barracks at Tamrack opened, and Constable Woods came in from searching the cabin of Clem Peters, who was under arrest for trapping out of season.

" Only a few pelts," he reported.

" Find anything else of interest?" demanded Corporal Steer.

Woods nodded; tossed a stoutly constructed envelope on the table.

" Yes," he said tersely. " Take a look at these."

Opening the envelope, Larry withdrew a wad of new-looking ten-dollar bills; examined them minutely through narrowed eyes.

" Forged!" he pronounced at last. " But as good workmanship as ever I've seen—they'd deceive anyone but an expert. But what's Clem doing with 'em? He's a ' hog ' trapper, all right, and I wouldn't put it past him to jump a claim if he thought he could get away with it. But I'd've sworn he's not mixed up with any counterfeiting gang."

Woods shook his head.

" No, there's nothing like that about Clem,"

he agreed. " The other way about, as a matter of fact—that ' slush ' was wished on him years ago in payment for a pokeful of gold—and he's been holding it ever since in the hope of finding the feller who swung it on him. The bills were put away with a lot of family papers in a box that didn't look as if it had been opened in years."

Larry locked the notes away in a drawer.

" Not the kind of thing to have knocking around, anyway," he said definitely. . . . " Especially when there's such a lot of it in Alaska these days—the U.S. marshal's right out for blood—thinks the feller who's passing the dud notes has crossed to this side, and has warned us to watch out for him. . . . Anything else stirring ?"

Woods nodded.

" Sure," he said, not too happily. " Dan Scales is back this side."

The corporal said something below his breath. In his periodical forays from over the Alaskan border, Scales gave more trouble than any ten of the local " bad-men " put together; card-sharp, hooch-pedlar, claim-salter, and up to now, with quite considerable justification, cocker of snooks at the Royal Canadian Mounted. For though the corporal had been gunning after him for more than two years as assiduously as a dog follows aniseed, always the Alaskan had waited until the last possible moment, and then slipped back over the border before the last half ounce of proof against him could be assembled.

" I'll get that cheap crook if it costs me my stripes," Larry promised viciously. " Any complaints of bad money, incidentally?"

Woods nodded again.

" Seems to have broken out in a fresh place," he reported. " Couple of days ago, Front Man was fingering a ten-dollar bill outside Barry Stokes's store, when up came Dan Scales. He asked to have a look at the bill, did a bit of the " quickness of the 'and " business, and returned the Injun only a one-spot—swore blind it was only a one-spot Front Man had handed him. I believe the Ojibway, of course, but there's no way of proving it."

A far-away look in suddenly narrowed eyes, the corporal shook his head.

" No, there's no proving it," he agreed slowly. " Just one man's word against another—if you can call Dan a man. . . . Harry Lorne's paying Treaty Money at eleven to-morrow," he added, with apparent inconsequence, and the constable's face brightened.

" Good!" he approved, for he liked to assist the Indian agent at the handing over of that inducement to the tribes to stay on Reservation.

Then his eyes, too, hardened. " I'll bet that's why Dan Scales is here," he exclaimed confidently. " There'll be plenty of loose cash flying around for the next couple of weeks, and that's what he's out for."

There was the slur of moccasined feet on the veranda outside. High cheek-boned, lank-haired, and, according to his lights, a good friend of the corporal's, Pot-a-Pie glided in. Though he stood expressionlessly before the desk until he was addressed, Larry knew that something had happened to upset him.

" What's the best news from you, Chief?" he demanded practically, after the usual exchange of greetings.

The Ojibway's slim shoulders rose and fell perceptibly, and the fingers of either hand moved by a bare half-inch.

" It is written that if the Fork-Tongued One comes on my Reserve again, there are those among the tribes who will make sure it is for the last time," he said tonelessly in Ojibway.

If Larry's heart took a leap into his throat, his manner was unperturbed as he replied in the same tongue.

" What's Scales done now he hasn't been doing this twenty years, anyway?" he demanded practically, and again there was that slight but eloquent gesture from the chief.

"One drop of falling water," he replied gravely, "the earth is able to drink and forget. Even ten score drops, and all to show is the rock where a little of the moss has been washed away. But "—the chief's jaw-muscles tightened —"if that dropping continues ceaselessly, moon by moon, in all seasons, there comes a moment when the rock itself wears thin."

More impressed than he allowed to appear, Larry nodded. In face of this clearly expressed warning, he had no difficulty in realizing that the sooner the Alaskan got out and stayed out the better would be his chance of survival. The trouble was, however, that living exclusively on bluff himself, the Alaskan would reject any warning as being inspired only by that same quality.

"You mean the tribe have decided it's time Dan called it a day?" he asked curtly.

On the point of spitting symbolically, remembering where he was, the chief checked himself in time.

"That Fork-Tongued One!" he snarled. "In the dead days, when the blood runs thin, he peddle what he say is fine hooch, though so that it may settle, it must be kept for the rising of two suns before it can be drunk. But the tribe say that when they take out the corks, it is to find not any hooch at all, but only tea and water."

Larry frowned. Though he had managed to suppress whisky peddling on the reservation to a large extent, he knew he would not be able to stamp it out altogether until he had put Dan Scales where he belonged. And as past experience had proved, that was not going to be easy.

" Serves your people right for buying it," the corporal said definitely, but ignoring this, the chief went on:

" Then, after Treaty Money was spent, so that all men need tobacco, and the women tea and sugar, he come again, that Fork-Tongued One, and this time took our best furs. But the tobacco for which we trade them had no savour, the tea no strength, nor the sugar sweetness. . . ."

So it went on, a catalogue of mean swindles and paltry thefts, so that Larry's only wonder was that the culprit was able still to move under his own power. And as, come what might, he was resolved that the peace of the reservation, unbroken now for half a generation, should be maintained, following a quick glance at Woods, he eyed the Ojibway fixedly, and leaned forward across the desk.

" I take it," he said levelly, " you want that sky-scraper over the border for good?"

The Indian returned the look intently, for never once had this *téotenny* [1] failed to keep faith.

[1] white man.

" If he is to go, it must be at once," the chief said definitely, and Larry nodded wholehearted agreement.

" Then listen, and if you heed what I say, never again will the tribe be troubled with the Fork-Tongued One," he said in the same level tone as before. " I take it you have, say, a dozen braves you can trust to do as you tell them?"

" A dozen score, if need be," Pot-a-Pie replied convincingly.

" Then listen again," Larry said, and spoke long and earnestly. . . .

Next day, the payment of Treaty Money was the usual affair of elaborate ceremonial in which the Indian delights. When the tribe filed back into camp, after a general exodus to the store for winter supplies, Larry was there as well, though of this only Pot-a-Pie was aware.

Full length within the gloom of the Chief's tepee, the corporal waited—and watched. Almost before he was expected, Dan Scales appeared— flabby-bodied, wide-faced, ingratiating, and obviously not too sure of his reception; with a cautious eye, too, for Front Man, whom he'd put one over the other morning with that ten-dollar bill.

But to the Alaskan's surprise, Front Man met him with a grave wave of the hand, and no evidence of ill-feeling. Obviously, Dan decided, the poor fish hadn't found out yet, and that was very much to the good.

And what was even better, there, sitting in his tepee entrance, staring contemplatively at the roll of money in his hand—what was left of his Treaty Money, apparently—was Calf Shirt, who in former transactions had been one of the most amenable, as he was one of the least resentful, of the tribe.

This, Scales decided happily, was going to be money for old rope.

He produced cigarettes, handed one to Calf Shirt, spoke boisterously of this and that, with the Ojibway responding with every sign of interest and good will.

"Treaty money?" Dan asked carelessly at last, when he felt the time was ripe, and indicating the currency Calf-Shirt was idly turning in his hand. Then, at the Ojibway's confirmatory nod: "Funny, them paying you in United States bills!" he added.

The Indian glanced at the money carelessly enough; shrugged indifferent shoulders. Then, to the Alaskan's delight, he passed it over for inspection.

If, like all the rest of him, Scales's hands were fat, they were uncommonly dexterous, and in the next few seconds their movement was not so much swift, as undetectable.

" Just the usual ten-spots," he said carelessly, folding the wad and handing it back to the incurious Ojibway, who stowed it somewhere on his person.

Scales left Calf Shirt after a few minutes, hoping devoutly that this first luck would hold —nine plunks to the good in the first quarter-hour was pretty good going. With the utmost care to keep out of sight of Pot-a-Pie, he wandered would-be carelessly between the lines of tepees.

The fervently wished-for luck did hold, as well, and all the more surprisingly because there was such a lot of money about; usually, after the necessary purchases of bacon and flour, tea and coffee, sugar and tobacco, what Treaty money remained went on any gosh-awful junk in the way of toys and candies that were coloured brightly enough to catch the eye. And though now, as usual, most of the tribe were flat broke, quite a number seemed still to have money to burn. . . . What was even better, with no real notion of its value. Like taking candy from kids—only that, luckily, Ojibways didn't holler same as kids did.

At last, sensitive fingers deep in his mackinaw pocket, Dan made the tally.

Thirty-two ten-dollar bills to the good, all traded for the one-dollar bills he'd substituted. At nine dollars a time profit, as near to five hundred dollars as made no difference. And, up to now, not a sign or kick from any one of the tribe. But as even Injuns were bound to get wise sooner or later, and then they'd put up a howl that'd be heard from here to a week on Wednesday, maybe he'd better scram—right now, while the going was good. . . .

With the trail in hard condition, he pulled in at the border Post in record time.

" Anything to declare, Dan?" asked Jack Wise, the custom-officer-cum-postmaster.

Dan hesitated for a moment. In the ordinary way, he'd have bluffed his way through, but it struck him that for some reason or other Jack was looking at him kind of funny. Better, p'raps, not to take a chance.

" Only this, Jack," he said, and showed a new skin handbag he'd bought in Dawson for his wife.

" Two dollars twenty to pay," pronounced the Customs' officer, taking the bill Scales produced from a bulging wallet.

It was then that Dan saw the funny look harden to something that wasn't funny at all. Still holding Scales with his glance, Wise made a sign, and a man stepped out of the cabin. A craggy man, with leathern face, boot-toe jaw, and enormous arms and shoulders. Who, taking the bill from Wise, examined it minutely through the magnifying glass he had brought from the cabin for the purpose.

" Let's be taking a peek at that wallet of yours, Dan," he said quietly at last, eyes and voice hard.

Though for the life of him he couldn't think what it could be, there was something here that didn't look too good to Scales, and he found his breath catching sharply in his throat.

" What's the big idea?" he cried protestingly at last.

" Hand over that wallet," the United States Marshal repeated purposefully. And when, sweating, the other had complied, following a careful inspection of each one of the bills it had contained, divided them into two separate piles, one of which he counted.

Then he laid a large and purposeful hand on Dan's shoulder.

" Daniel Scales," he said formally, " I arrest you on the charge of attempting to utter one counterfeit United States ten-dollar bill, and with being in illegal possession of thirty-one others of similar denomination. Upon information," he added less officially, " supplied over the wire by the Royal Canadian Mounted Police."

He might have added, and with equal truth, that the bills had been supplied by them as well.

But this, of course, he was not to know.

CHAPTER VI

Corporal Steer acts from Experience

Reassured after a swift backward glance to where the narrow, reed-bordered river flowed into the lake, Slim Lannigan swung the canoe unhandily to the beach. He landed, pulled the craft up the shingle, and under cover of the thickly-growing scrub, obliterated foot and canoe marks from the sand; collected pack and rifle. A moment later he was striking purposefully into the forest.

In a straight line three miles away was the Honeycomb country, where the trees thinned to a barren rock-bestrewn belt that, after half a mile or so, rose sharply to a cliff where there were caves—hundreds of them by all accounts. A man could lie up there, safe not only from ginger-headed Corporal Steer, who had been camping on his trail ever since that business at Abe Patterson's store, but free of all the Yellerlegs in the North.

A couple of months, say, until the hunt shifted, then a swift break to the Alaskan border. Once in United States territory, everything would be jake with the levers up.

Nevertheless, it had been nip-and-tuck to reach here far enough ahead of pursuit to cover his tracks, but now he'd made the grade, he knew enough to travel in a straight line through three miles of forest. The sun was high and strong, and there were breaks in the foliage overhead, so that even without the compass that had slipped overboard when he'd made that grab for the paddle to avoid sunken rocks ahead, it would be easy to keep direction.

Bad luck, though, that the going wasn't a bit easier; the ground was so thick with scrub and raspberry canes there was no forcing a way through —you had to pick out each step. However, the bushes sprang back into place as he passed, and so far as he could make out, left no trace. With one of the most expert trackers in the North camping so close on his trail, that was all to the good. Further, every now and then there were clearings, sunbathed, and easy to the feet, and these made a welcome break.

After a little, however, clouds gathered, and the sun went in, and without that guide you had to be a good trailsman to be sure of your direction. To make things worse, he struck muskeg, so that his moccasins grew black and soaked. With the humid, moisture-laden air, came the mosquitoes—not a few at a time, as in the prairie provinces, but in whirring clouds, avid and blood-hungry—and Slim's blood was as yet un-thinned by the North, and his skin unhardened.

Another circumstance that worked against him was that the trees had changed with the change of soil, the big-trunked hardwoods giving place to spruce and cedar and stunted tamrac, and all so closely growing that, with the branches inter-locked overhead, they shut out any sight of the sun, so that to keep his line it was necessary to make détour after détour. If, actually, he *was* keeping his line, and that he wasn't as sure of as he would have liked.

That, however, could be discovered for certain when he reached the heavily-timbered ground; there, the going would be both better and drier, and he would be able to take his bearings.

The trouble was, though, that fight his way through the tangle as he might, he did not seem to be making an awful lot of progress.

He took a pull on himself—above all things, he must not panic. To encourage himself for what lay ahead, he camped, made a meal, and—though speed was so very much the essence of the contract—rested for a full half-hour.

Heartened, he set off again. But though he fought his way resolutely through the tangle, still there was no sign of higher ground.

Then, suddenly, narrow face tense, deeply-set eyes fearful, he stopped dead; sniffed hard at the humid air that carried the reek of wood smoke.

Was this the Yellerlegs who, tracking him, had overrun the trail?

Warily Slim cast about the soddened ground until he found a footprint. Comparatively freshly made, as well—and pointing in the direction from where came that scent of smoke. Soundlessly, he approached.

Yes; there, dully glowing, was the remains of a fire. But whoever made it had gone on, for there was no one within sight, nor any sign of stores or camp equipment.

He was moving forward to make a closer inspection, when suddenly his stride faltered. Immediately in the forefront of those that lined the tiny clearing, that beach tree with the scarred bark, as if it had been gnawed by some animal or other, struck a note of familiarity.

The fire reached, Slim's breath caught sharply in his throat, and his heart pounded. Not Yellerlegs' camp, but his own, that he had left only an hour or so before. When he came to make the test, the footprints were his own as well.

He stood for a moment to regain self-control. Nothing to be scared about, he told himself—the very best trailsmen lost directions sometimes. The higher ground was still where it had been, and he knew the general direction. Very well then, it was only a question of taking more care.

He set off again, more deliberately this time, and with a keen eye for landmarks, so that progress was slower, even, than before. And two hours later he was back at the camp again.

There was a cold feeling at the pit of his stomach as he started out again, more quickly, this time, thrusting bull-like through the all-pervading entanglement, though pausing expediently at intervals to calculate direction. If he was to make the grade at all, third time would have to be lucky.

It was when he was congratulating himself that he had made real progress, that, with a sharp stab of familiarity, he caught the gleam of dulled silver above the surrounding scrub. A dozen more steps, and he saw that it was the beech tree that overlooked the camp; that for the third time he was back at his starting-place.

In what, after all, is not an unusual situation, the real trailsman would have called it a day, rekindled his fire, and, after a meal, turned in for the night to steady overwrought nerves, and the hope of a sight of the early morning sun on awakening. But Slim was a Saskatchewan desert rat,[1] accustomed only to the open prairie, and he had that on his mind that makes for panic.

For the next twenty-four hours it was as if that cold camp fire was a magnet, irresistibly

[1] Desert rat—Plainsman.

strong, and he the needle. Time and time again he set out, sometimes slowly and with a numb deliberation, at others, gulping, thigh muscles quivering, to plunge frenziedly through the tangle. But only, self-defeated by ignorance, sooner or later to find himself back at the camp again.

This was the time when he should have taken stock of his surroundings. So close to the magnetic North, distrustful of a compass, and independent of the sun, your real path-finder banks only on his own intensive observation, a photographic memory for each yard of the way, to correct the universal tendency to turn in his tracks, and his own perfected experience. He knows that it is the northern side of a tree where the bark is thickest and the rings closest together; that due to the prevailing winds, the tree tops on exposed places lean to the north-east. Slim, however, knew only that he was lost.

Night had fallen when he left that sinister base for the last time. Half an hour or so of aimless plunging, and he fell sprawling; and there lay exhausted until he awakened to sunshine and the singing of birds. Refreshed, to an extent heartened, though still trepidous, he breakfasted sparsely, took his bearings once more, and set off in what, this time, he knew to be the right direction.

It was about ten o'clock that the scrub thinned to woodland; less than a hundred yards, and the trees grew close again, so that he lost sight of the sun. Another quarter of an hour, and he was lost beyond hope of recovery.

That day was an accentuation of the nightmare of the afternoon before—a time of aimless beating between the trees, of the slow, awful, recognition of landmarks he had passed minutes or hours before; of wandering in wide arcs or smaller circles. And all about him teemed the life of the forest—uninterested—as unheeding of him as it was preoccupied with its own destiny.

Towards night, however, the forest and its people grew less impersonal.

The whisky-jacks, those cheerful and ubi-quitous birds who rob the prospector of stores and temper, grew less friendly; grouped and mocked together, whisked derisively at the sweat-ing stumbling figure; the far-carrying ventri-loquial cry of the loon was mocking and derisive too; the bright-eyed squirrels overhead chattering contempt; tree-stumps, shattered by age or tempest, took form, menacing him, and seeming to bar his way. The whole forest was alive with antagonism.

Overcome, he slept at last, awakening to dark-ness and a blacker nightmare even than those that had infested his dreams. The bullet-wound in the temple, blue-rimmed, with the thin runnel of blood down the cheek as Slim had left him slumped on the store-house floor, everywhere about him was Abe Patterson. Staring sightlessly from the foliage, advancing on him from between the tree trunks, barring his passage across the clearing.

Sometimes he was there singly, stalking at Slim's side; sometimes in duplicate; at others everywhere, hundreds of him; in every tree, approaching him from all directions; before him and, when he looked fearfully over his shoulder, stealing on him from behind.

Then, for periods of varying lengths, Abe would not be there at all, so that, cursing himself for having given way to imagination, Slim would persuade himself that the illusion had passed. And then, suddenly, from behind a tree trunk, or flitting ghost-like across the drive ahead—there Abe would be again.

Slim suffered terribly, too, from thirst, for there were no streams running through the forest. There was the pitcher plant growing all about the swamps, each one filled with a good half-cupful of clear water, but in his ignorance this Slim did not know, so that he drank only what he was able to squeeze precariously from the muskeg; brown, slimy, and malodorous. There was still plenty of food in his pack, but his tongue was too swollen, and his throat and gums too dry, to eat it.

That night, which, to avoid the closed-in feeling, he spent in the middle of a tiny clearing, was worse, even, than the day.

It was the Spirits of the Dead at Play, as the Ojibway term the Northern Lights. High up, the arc of heaven was a dark uniform blue, changeless, immovable, and in awe-inspiring contrast to the vivid and diaphanous colours that swirled and eddied below. To Slim, physically feverish and mentally prostrate, imagination aflame, this was horror piled on horror.

With the centre as clear as the long-disputed ground between two contending armies, like hosts lining up for battle, shifting a little here and there, but under discipline, the Spirits—luminous with every shade and gradation of the primary colours—would assemble north and south—or east and west, Slim did not know which.

Then, as at a given signal, the two masses would hurl irresistibly forward, to intermingle full-centre in raging, surging, battle, the colours more unearthly even than before because more luminous, intermingling in the frenzy of combat, until it was as if the whole vault of heaven was one huge battle-ground. Then, at last—again as if at a signal—each side would withdraw, straggling across, each to its own base, there slowly to reform before joining issue again.

Even though Slim had been in the North long enough for the display to have become a commonplace, there was an element in this that, before the pageant dissolved in the first flush of dawn, brought a horror that left him grey-faced, stare-eyed and semi-delirious. In some impalpable fashion, in each of those contending armies every gradation of colour formed itself into a face, bloodstreaked, in whose forehead was a tiny, blue-rimmed wound . . . .

Before the sun was high he moved off, though in what direction he neither knew nor cared; except that it had disbanded the Dance of the Dead Man, the sun had ceased to interest him, as had everything but to escape from himself. Semi-starved now, consumed with thirst, he had no strength to walk upright, nor even to brush away the mosquitoes that settled on him in clouds. Progress, such as it was, degenerated to a phantom-ridden crawl.

It was high noon when, only half-consciously, he saw that the trees had thinned out; between the trunks ahead caught the glint of sunlight on water. The lake, that he had left—how many ageless days ago? But where he could drink— and drink—and go on drinking.

Panting, swollen tongue protruding, he reached the shingle at a palm-and-knee shuffle.

A Stetson-hatted figure, on the collar of whose

mackinaw was the buffalo-head badge of the Royal Canadian Mounted Police, stepped out from the shade of the trees; stood looking not unpitifully on that abjectly broken figure.

"I want you, Slim," said Corporal Steer quietly.

Slowly, painfully, as if it outweighed him, Slim lifted his head.

"But not so much as I want *you*!" he gasped, and collapsed face-downward in the shingle.

"Queer—the way a lost man always walks in circles, so that he comes back to the point he started from," Larry muttered, as he rendered first aid to his prisoner.

CHAPTER VII

Corporal Steer deals with Rebellion

Said the Provincial Minister concerned, to McNeill, in awarding him the contract to make the road from Lake Nawidjawaulk to Brackwater River:

" One thing you've got to steer clear of is trouble with the Indians. And let me tell you, there's a bunch of free Crees around that area who're going to regard the advancing tide of progress same as if it was a plague-wave."

McNeill waved this aside as habitually he brushed aside anything that threatened his own convenience.

" I've never yet met the Indian a couple of cakes of chewin' plug an' an order for a pair of moccasins wouldn't have eatin' out of my hand," he said truculently, for he was that kind of man.

The Minister, however, had something yet to say.

" Listen, Charlie," he said purposefully. " There have been signs and portents lately that've occasioned us considerable uneasiness, and it's our policy to see there's nothing that can be seized on by the tribes as an excuse for trouble. And old Chief, Sounding Thunder and his Crees have been around those parts so long they've come to regard that neck of the woods as their own property. Their ancestral home, if you know what I mean."

"Then I guess it's up to me to show 'em different," McNeill said promptly.

The Minister frowned.

"The only thing that's up to you," he said definitely, "is to instruct your gang that the first clash with Sounding Thunder sees the cancellation of your contract. And I don't mean maybe, or even very likely."

M'Neill was startled—and showed it.

"But look," he cried, "when you say——"

"Particularly," continued the Minister, "as old Sounding Thunder spent the winter before last, *and* the one before that, on the ' woodpile '.[1] And if it hadn't been that it was thought expedient to ignore him, he'd have eaten his Christmas dinner behind the bars last year as well."

"Do you mean to tell me," shouted McNeill, " that——"

"So," the Minister proceeded, as if at a sudden happy thought, " if we could show we'd closed down on important public works rather than

[1] Jail.

encroach on the immemorial haunts of our Red Brother, it'd be a pretty good gesture, don't you think?"

"I certainly do *not*," McNeill said swiftly, and stuffed his copy of the contract into his despatch case.

. . . .

As work on the new road progressed, it seemed to Tom Mullins, the foreman, that the Indians were more taciturn even than was customary. And though he had given strict orders as to their treatment, he had to admit the return in affability was meagre. While no Cree refused a cake of plug tobacco or a handful of cigarettes, always acceptance was with a scowl instead of a smile.

"We're about as welcome with that bunch of Crees as a circular from the Incorporated Society of Embalmers at a Home for Incurables," he complained to Jake Flynn, an old trustie who had worked with him on every outfit in the last twenty years.

That disillusioned veteran sniffed.

"The only way to treat an Injun is rough," he said. "Spoon-feed 'em, an' all you get for thanks is trouble."

Bill nodded.

"That's what we're going to have this trip," he said pessimistically. "I can feel it comin'."

So, apparently, could the gang in general,

who were worried by the groups of Indians who stood silently watching them at work. And when, to avoid muskeg, it was necessary to depart ever further from the trail, and the Crees became still more persistent, they were not shy in putting up a kick about it.

" I give you fair warnin'," Jake Flynn complained to Mullins, " that if those Crees aren't called off pretty soon, the boys'll get busy moving 'em. S'matter of fact, it's been all I could do to hold 'em back already."

Tom looked at him in horror.

" Lay off talk of that kind, for the love of *Mike*!" he cried. " Don't you realize that just one squeal from that bunch of Crees, an' McNeill an' his contract get thrown to the wolves?"

" That's what I'd like to see happen to those Injuns," Jake remarked feelingly.

But the farther the road penetrated into the woods, the more Crees showed up to hamper the work. And then one day, when the road had reached a natural clearing in the woods, bang across the survey line was the Indian camp; tepees, huskies, horses, squaws, papooses. Smoking at the entrance of his tent, a survey peg on either hand, was old Chief Sounding Thunder himself.

" *Now* what'll we do?" Flynn demanded blankly of Tom Mullins, who succeeded in hiding his trepidation as a good leader should.

"Soon's the old buzzard sees he's in the way, he'll move all right, don't you worry," he said unconvincingly.

"An' if not?" Jake demanded.

"In that case, I guess I'll have to talk to him myself," Tom responded, registering the confidence he didn't feel.

He had every excuse for pessimism. The four cakes of plug tobacco he selected as overture to negotiations were accepted with disparagement, as were the tins of bully, the two pounds of coffee, and the carton of sugar.

"Now beat it from my woods," said Sounding Thunder, who was of advanced middle age and paunch.

Tom shook his head.

"Can't do that, Chief," he said, hoping he did not look as angry as he felt. "We're on Government contract, and if we don't carry the work out to time we'll all be shot at dawn, or somethin'. Sorry, an' all that, but I gotter ask you to strike camp."

Chief Sounding Thunder's only response to this was to give a sign to the braves who lined either side of the survey pegs, and who for the most part were carrying rifles or shot-guns.

In response to those silent instructions, they began to encircle the gang as they worked.

Slowly at first, but with increasing velocity, in single file and silence, almost imperceptibly the ring closed in.

Towards midday, McNeill showed up, redder in the face, and more truculent than ever. Sounding Thunder made another of those signs, and suddenly the day was filled with clamour.

Though McNeill was reckoned a scrapper of eminence, now, though he tried not to show it, he was pretty badly scared.

"What," he demanded of Sounding Thunder, his voice steadier than his hands, "is the big idea? This isn't Indian Reservation, and well you know it."

The old chief shrugged gaunt, indifferent shoulders.

"Reserve or not," he replied imperturbably, "it was given to my people by the Great White Spirit more moons since than there are cicadas in the trees. If they are not left in peace, I fear for what they may do, for they are young, with the blood hot in their veins."

The blood was hot in McNeill's veins as well, and this time he made no bones about showing it.

"You old four-flusher," he shouted; "you know as well as I do that you've only to give the order to shift that tent of yours, an' the whole bunch'll follow like huskie dogs a trail of aniseed."

Slant eyes expressionless, Sounding Thunder settled himself more comfortably in his blanket.

" If you uproot the ancient tree," he said calmly, " then will it surely die. Soon will come the Month of the Frozen Moon,[1] with the Wild Women,[2] to eat into the bones of the ancient as the skinning-knife into the kill. And I am too old to take the trail."

" The only trail you're ast to take," McNeill pointed out excitedly, " is a coupler hundred yards the other side of this survey."

" *Téotenny* it is who will take the trail," Sounding Thunder observed ominously.

There was a shattering detonation of firearms; a hail of bullets whistled over the heads of the gang. Yelling, leaping, circling, the Crees fired volley after volley—each trajectory a shade lower than the one before.

A lesser man than McNeill would have been glad to call it a day. Yet, though as scared as a man may be, he held on.

" Best thing is to get in touch with the Minister," advised Tom Mullins, ducking hastily to a bullet that hummed five or six feet above his head.

McNeill's idea, however, soared higher even than that.

" For all we know," he pointed out, " this may

[1] November.   [2] Wild Women = Hurricanes.

be a match that's going to set the whole Indian people alight. I'm appealing direct to the Governor-General."

In his office-cum-orderly room at the log-built barracks at Tamrack it was with an expression of amazement that Larry turned from the telephone to his opposite number.

" Brackwater," he said, " have had a message from Division that they've had a message from Headquarters at Ottawa that they've had a message from the Government that they've had a report from an authoritative source that an Indian rising is on the point of breaking out at Nawidjawaulk portage." He paused. " Now *what* d'you know about that?" he added.

Woods thought for a moment before his hard-bitten face cleared.

" That old scrimshanker Sounding Thunder, for a million dollars!" he cried, and Larry nodded.

" I'll say it is," he agreed, saddled his mare, and rode the dozen odd miles to the scene of conflict.

Emerging into the clearing, it was to discover the road gang the huddled axis of a rapidly rotating wheel of Cree Indians. And though the firing had died away some time before, immediately with his appearance, and prefaced by yells of derision, the volley was the heaviest yet.

A deflated McNeill hurried to meet him.

"Where are the rest of you?" he shouted, but until he had reined up alongside the panting contractor, Larry made no reply.

"What may be the trouble, anyway?" he said shortly, and McNeill explained with forensic elaboration.

"What're you, anyway—a scout in advance of the party?" he demanded at the finish.

"*And* the main body and rearguard," said Larry, who had dropped his reins and was rolling a cigarette.

"But—but—" McNeill stammered, with an apprehensive eye on the savagely gyrating Crees, "you'll need a full troop at least."

"All I'll need," Larry replied unpleasantly, urging the mare towards the Chief, "is to keep my blinking temper!"

"Howdy, Yellerlegs!" Sounding Thunder greeted him, but refraining from meeting the constabulary eye.

Larry glanced at his wrist-watch.

"I'll give you just five minutes," he said coldly, "to shift that tent."

Sounding Thunder's response was to expel tobacco juice to within inches of the mare's forefoot.

"And if I stay?" he questioned.

"Why, then," Larry said, "I shall arrest you for obstructing and interfering with a police officer in the execution of his duty. With your record, you know what that'll mean."

It has to be said for Chief Sounding Thunder that he did not hesitate.

"I stay," he decided uncompromisingly.

Of all McNeill's life, probably the longest five minutes was when, abandoning their gyrations in favour of ringside seats, the tribe crowded round for the dénouement—a period wherein the chirping of the cicadas in the trees was the only sound to break the stillness.

At last came the moment when Larry threw his leg over the saddle; dismounted. Brushing past Sounding Thunder, he entered the tent, and kicked out the centre-pole, so that the whole contraption collapsed. Unmolested, he took the same course with the three or four others that obstructed the right-of-way. As they, too, fell, he pitched them clear of the survey line.

"Carry on with the work," he said curtly to McNeill; and to Sounding Thunder, "Come right along, you old moron, and if you get off with three months you'll be luckier than you deserve."

Deliberately, eyes glinting, Chief Sounding Thunder stood up.

"Three months no good," he said definitely, and counted on his fingers. "Eight moons I stay with you. Three years since—two years

since—all the Dead Months I was in the tie-up.
There I had warmth, all the meat I could eat,
and because I am old, not any-much work. But
last year, when with the falling of the leaf I go
Bad Man again, no one give any heed, so that
all the Dead Months I shiver in my tepee,
starving on rabbit."

He paused.

" But this year, because I am old and needful
of rest, I make no mistake," he added, and
kicked Larry violently on the shin.

CHAPTER VIII

Corporal Steer effects a Rescue

It was a week ago that, unheralded and unexplained, the Englishman's canoe decanted him into Lurgan's Landing, and his subsequent movements had been watched and discussed with a curiosity that had become only more active the longer it remained unsatisfied.

If he was a tourist, why, they asked, instead of "snoopin' around" in the aimless way he did, was he making no effort to hire a guide? If in want of a job, why hadn't he gone right after one? If a prospector, why hadn't he hit the trail?

It was in Tom Long's Chinese Eats Parlour that the mystery became explained, and the notoriously direct methods of Sourdough Bryan that extracted the solution. When Sourdough came in to supper, the only vacant seat in the room was at the Englishman's table, and into this the old-timer incontinently lowered himself.

He chatted for a few moments, and then, no information forthcoming, said:

"Listen, stranger. What do you aim to do, here in the North?"

The Englishman replied unhesitatingly, in the slow drawl that from the first had been the cause of so much amusement to the populace:

" I'm going to find Sergeant Sheridan," he said levelly.

For a moment Sourdough regarded him open-mouthed. Already three expertly-manned expeditions had returned empty from a search that in each case had extended even to the Barren Land itself. A moment, and addressing the room at large, he waved a calloused hand towards his *vis-à-vis*.

" Boys," he shouted, " take a look at the bold an' intrepid pioneer who aims to blaze the trail to Sergeant Sheridan!"

Momentarily the talk and laughter stopped. One or two comments, pitying or mildly derogatory, were shouted back before the room settled down again. Now the stranger's presence was explained, with one exception no one seemed particularly interested.

The exception was the boy—twenty-one, or so, the Englishman judged, and, like himself, a stranger to the town—of whose presence at the next table to his own he had all along been so vividly aware.

Watching him unobtrusively, he saw that his face had turned suddenly pale beneath his tan. And as their glances met, eyes blazing, body rigid, the boy pushed back his chair and was beside him.

" And who do you think'll go seek *you*—when you don't come back?" he demanded contemptuously.

The Englishman looked at him speculatively.

" What makes you think I'm as helpless as all that?" he asked quietly.

Slowly the boy surveyed him from feet to head and, more slowly, back again.

" Because," he said, his voice venomous, " it takes more than a cissy cheechako[1] who couldn't find the hole in a doughnut to break trail across The Barrens."

The Englishman looked at him for a moment.

" What makes you think Sheridan got as near to Hudson Bay as that?" he inquired interestedly, and saw the boy's eyes waver as, with another contemptuous shrug, he turned away.

" Bradwell don't love you any, I guess," Sourdough remarked, as the door closed behind the boy, and he pointed to the place the other had left—. " He ain't even through with his supper!"

About two o'clock the next morning, while Lurgan's Landing was still white beneath the moon, the Englishman loaded his canoe, and

[1] cheechako = tenderfoot.

within a few minutes was breasting the slow-moving Saskatchewan River.

But it was not until the first flush of dawn pearled the eastern horizon that he saw, on the left, the gleam of a newly-lighted camp-fire, and so swung his tiller over and nosed his canoe toward the bank. As he shut off his engine, the uncertain figure, cooking breakfast over a cedar-wood fire, rose and came to the bank to meet him.

" Sorry!" the Englishman said hastily, for the camper was the boy with whom he had had the passage of arms in Tom Long's. Nor, from his tone, had his opinion of the other changed in the meantime.

" What's the big idea—you horning in on me like this?" he demanded curtly.

" Not thinking it necessary to use my night-glasses," the Englishman said quietly, " I'd no idea who you were "—and scored by questioning the other's obedience to the code by which no camper may refuse hospitality to the passer-by.

" You'd need stronger lenses than any night-glasses to read the ' welcome ' sign on any camp of mine," the boy said uncompromisingly.

" In that case, I'd better push on," the English-man returned cheerfully.

Until about seven that evening he travelled without rest; then he landed at a place where the trees grew down to the water, cached his canoe, and after a cold supper, slept dreamlessly.

It was six o'clock in the morning when he passed from the Saskatchewan River into the first of the chain of lakes through which lay the chief part of the journey. He chose one of the innumerable islands with which the lake was studded, cached his canoe in a bed of reeds, waded ashore, took cover, and waited.

At ten he heard the distant throb of an outboard engine, and half an hour later, having rounded the point where the river flowed into the lake, Bradwell's canoe passed. The Englishman did not follow until it had disappeared around the bend of one of the other islands.

For the next four days he was careful to keep an island between them. At night, from the one in the rear of that chosen by Bradwell, he kept watch on the camp-fire.

Towards late afternoon on the fifth day, however, he missed him. All that sweltering, airless morning, until well after Bradwell had camped for the midday meal, there had been no difficulty in keeping him under observation. Then the Englishman was obliged to wait so long to allow the boy undisturbed passage of a stretch of river that connected two of the lakes, that when he followed, the other canoe had passed out of sight.

He hesitated. Had Bradwell gone on to the farther lake, or camped on one of the islands?

On the whole, he thought it better to wait until
dark, and then paddle quietly across in the hope
of detecting the other's camp-fire. Meantime, he
pushed well into the cover of the wood, and
cooked his first hot meal of the trip.

The night, that was of the same brooding,
airless heat as the day, fell with the suddenness
of the North. Venturing into the open, the
Englishman glanced anxiously to the sky, and
what he saw was not reassuring.

Now he travelled at full speed. Luckily there
were only four islands in this particular lake. He
made the circuit of the first without any of his
previous efforts towards concealment. At any cost
it was necessary he should find Bradwell.

He passed on to the second island, and the
third, but with no result. Then, as the moon
was obscured and did not seem likely to re-
appear, he shouted and kept on shouting. No
reply came.

Half a mile ahead from the last of the islands,
where, from the fringe, he could discover no trace
of his quarry, the lake joined another stretch of
the river before again linking up with open
water. And as it was apparent Bradwell had
pressed forward, and now there would be no time
to reach him, he decided to land, hoping to
Heaven the other, also, had been able to read the
signs.

Skirting the shore for half a mile, he took his observations—that were unusually satisfactory—and then chugged back to a beach of hard firm sand where, backed as this was by trees, there would be plenty of kindling. There was time for a meal, anyway, though it would have to be a quick one.

He landed, trudged up the slope—and stumbled over something that sat up with a jerk and a little strangled cry.

"Hello—spy!" exclaimed a voice that was vibrant with antagonism.

"Oh, you're there, are you?" the Englishman said, for the moment too startled and thankful to think of anything better.

In the murk of that breathless, expectant night, Bradwell's face shone clear-cut and sullen.

"What's the big idea—following me?" he demanded.

The Englishman shrugged his shoulders.

"This is a pretty wide country," he fended. "Also a free—even if before long it's going to be a pretty dangerous—one."

Bradwell made a gesture of contempt for the evasion.

"And who *are* you, anyway?" he demanded curtly.

The Englishman shrugged his shoulders.

"Just a cissy cheechako who couldn't find the

hole in a doughnut," he reminded him, and saw with interest, not untinctured with admiration, the boy's effort at self-control.

"Come clean," Bradwell said tersely. "Tell me why you're camping on my trail?"

The Englishman returned the glance with one as direct.

"Because your trail is the one that's going to lead me to Sergeant Sheridan," he said quietly; and almost before the Englishman realized it, Bradwell had sprung to his feet, and, eyes blazing was facing him.

"Just let me give you one piece of advice," he said, speaking each word slowly and distinctly. "Go back. I'm not arguing; I'm telling you. Go right back where you belong." Adding, below his breath, as he half-turned away, "It'll be healthier."

From the sullen, low-lying indigo overhead came the rumble of thunder, and the Englishman said with a quick but quiet efficiency that seemed to take Bradwell by surprise:

"And it'll be healthier for both of us to get right away from this particular spot."

Before Bradwell had time to protest, the Englishman seized his wrist in a grip from which in any case he could not have released himself, and hurried down to the water-edge.

"Where is your canoe?" he said shortly.

Bradwell wrenched himself free.   A further movement, incredibly quick, and the Englishman was looking into the muzzle of an automatic.

" Lay hands on me again," the boy said in a voice unsteady with anger, " and you'll be a very dead man."

The Englishman made a gesture, weary but impatient.

" Talking about dying," he said, " if you don't want to pass out very soon and very unpleasantly yourself, you'll help instead of hampering."

There must have been something arresting in his manner, for as if involuntarily, Bradwell lowered the pistol, gazing at him uncertainly.

" What do you mean ?" he asked.

The Englishman indicated the lowering sky, and inhaled a long deep breath of the stifling air.

" Can't you read the signs ?   Feel it coming ?" he asked.

In the moment before Bradwell replied, they seemed to be enfolded by a silence wherein there was cessation, complete and somehow breathless, of every natural sound. Not a leaf stirred among the branches; the lake spread before them black and motionless; all the stirrings of furred and feathered things, that with those northern nights bring a sense of companionship, had died away; even the ever-present, high-pitched call of the loon had merged into the universal hush. It was as if the earth waited with suspended breath for something tremendous and inevitable. And in that brief hiatus Bradwell was brought to the realization of what impended.

" You mean——?" he said jerkily, his face white and newly fearful against the darkness.

The Englishman nodded.

" Yes," he said shortly. " *Yootin Wetikoo*." And then again, " Where's your canoe?"

" Cached in the scrub here to the left," Bradwell replied quickly, and the other saw with relief how completely he had reacted to their situation.

" I'll go and get it," the Englishman said. He knew it was heavily laden with stores, and because less encumbered, his own was lighter. " Jump into mine and head for the cliff on your right," he instructed. " There are caves there. Make for the nearest, and show me a light." He thrust his torch into Bradwell's hand, and, as he hesitated, " Don't argue—do as I tell you. I'll follow, right enough."

" Leave my canoe to take care of itself," Bradwell pleaded, but the Englishman shook his head.

" No. They'll need the stores," he said, and was conscious of Bradwell's sudden intake of breath.

The Englishman found the Peterboro' where, in similar circumstances, he would have chosen to hide it. Bradwell had driven in, head on, into a natural tunnel formed by a bank of clay and the scrub that overhung it, so that it was necessary to fend the heavily-laden craft stern first to open water. This took time, and experience told the Englishman how vital, now, was every instant.

The engine took half a dozen turns before it fired, and then it was necessary to curve in a wide sweep to head in the right direction. A guiding beam of light from some height ahead told him that Bradwell, at least, had found sanctuary.

Torch in hand, the Englishman discovered him waiting at a low flat rock, to where his canoe was moored.

" There's a natural path between the boulders back here," he reported. " Half-way up, the cliff face is honeycombed with caves. I've chosen one."

" Help me up with the canoe," the Englishman said shortly—and even as he spoke the storm broke.

One instant the sky was a dark sullen indigo; the next, from horizon to horizon, a livid sheet of slate-blue, from which shot jagged spear-points of lightning that, with the irregular flickering of a badly-projected film, silhouetted and died and

resilhouetted the outline of spruce and tamrack
on the mainland bank.

Then, instantaneously, came the cataclysmic
roar of thunder. From that moment it was as if
the very skies were in process of disintegration;
peal followed upon peal and roar merged into roar,
the one breaking into its predecessor before being
drowned by the one that followed.

It was not possible to speak; even thought
seemed swamped. Gripping himself, the Englishman seized the bow thwart of his canoe, and half
lifted it to the natural jetty. Nerve bruised but
unbroken, Bradwell bent to the stern thwart,
motioned their route, and swung the torch in a
wide arc to guide their way.

The path sloped steeply between the encroach-
ing boulders, so that negotiation was both difficult
of accomplishment and costly as to time. Half-
way to the summit, however, the cliff side was
broken by a natural platform, the face pierced
here and there with caves, and they negotiated
the canoe into the nearest.

Simultaneously with this, the lightning and the
thunder ceased as instantaneously as if their
motive-power had been turned off from a switch-
board. Where, before, the world had been one
vast crescendo of sound, now there descended a
silence that had in it a strange sense of prepara-
tion; as if the storm had been designed only to

clear the stage for a tragedy to which the fiercely burning woods on the mainland was only the fitting prelude.

White-faced, but his spirit rising triumphant over fear, Bradwell turned to descend for the salvaging of his own canoe. But with a quick hand on his arm, the Englishman forced him into the cave that had been chosen for their refuge. There, side by side, they lay prone.

From far to the south had come a sound like the rumble of heavy distant traffic, but in it a curious note of lament, and the Englishman glanced anxiously at the forest fire.

" Pray Heaven it doesn't face this way," he said in a low voice, and was conscious of the shudder that ran through the boy at his side.

Cumulatively, the note of lament took dominance over the traffic sounds until the effect was of a moaning, that, beginning far down the register, ascended gradually higher and louder until it came as the blended sirens of a thousand ships. Louder, louder yet, and still more loud; nearer, and yet more near. It was as if the whole world was shrieking in torment.

Then it was upon them! Before their eyes, the lake seemed literally to lift into the air, and though it was a hundred feet below, the spray from that lashed and tortured water swirled and eddied about them as on a beach in storm.

As the Devil Wind struck, the forest glowed
incandescent as a blacksmith's forge. Whole
trees, burning fiercely, were either uprooted or
broken off, to be hurled along like beacons against
the purple sky. Dislodged rocks of inconceivable
size tossed about like toy balloons; caught by
the onrush, Bradwell's canoe somersaulted out of
sight, the bales and packages that were its cargo
speeding like bullets into the distance.

Characteristically, like the charge of devils in
column, the course of *Yootin Wetikoo* was a clearly
defined path, with the areas to right and left
untouched. And as the roar of an express train
diminishes with its passing, soon the fury died
to the first moaning, and so to the silence of
accomplishment.

After that, deluge. The rain came not in
sheets, but as with the turning-on of a million
taps, in solid rods of water that rechurned the
smoothened lake to hissing, leaping froth, and
that, because the Devil Wind had left spaces the
flames could not bridge, swamped to sizzling
impotency the smouldering stumps of what once
had been the forest.

Half an hour the flood lasted before, quite
suddenly, it died. Within a few minutes the
sky cleared, and the moon, swinging above the
tree tops, shone refulgently on a wounded but
freshened world.

There had been so long a silence that, turning slowly to discover the boy's head buried deeply in his arms, the Englishman thought that, exhausted, he was asleep. But, as though instinctively aware of his glance, Bradwell stirred; lifted his face so that it was quite close to his own. And the Englishman saw then that the conflagration on the opposite bank was not the only fire that had suddenly been quenched, nor the storm of which they had been spectators, and so nearly the victims, the only one to have died away.

Bradwell's face, drawn and white in the whiter moonlight, was fear-filled; his lips trembled into a half-ironic smile.

" And I thought you a cheechako!" he said feelingly.

" How do you know I'm not?" the Englishman asked; and the boy rose to his feet.

" Don't hedge," he said shortly. " Is a cheechako able to read the signs of *Yootin Wetikoo*— that comes only once every five years or so?" He had been speaking while brushing the sand and debris from his clothing, but now, in the direct fashion that appealed to the Englishman quite a lot, looked up to face him. " But for you I'd have been dead," he said, and shuddered with the remembrance of those hurtling rocks and tree trunks. " And *how*!" he added. " Me—I only thought it heading up for an ordinary storm!"

The Englishman made no reply.

" How did *you* know?" Bradwell demanded at last, breaking into the silence.

" I've seen it before," the Englishman said indifferently, and the boy looked at him searchingly.

" Here—in the North?" he asked abruptly.

Rather shamefacedly, the other nodded.

" Yes," he said, and paused, frowning. " You know darned well I'm a Mounted Policeman," he accused; and Bradwell, in turn, nodded.

" It struck me in Tom Long's you might be," he acknowledged. " Somehow there's a Mountie look about you. That's why I came over to your table and started ' stringing ' you—just to find out. But even then you fooled me—or at any rate I wasn't sure. So I pulled out straight away, and travelled with my ear to the trail. The only thing *was* to try and make a clean getaway."

He grinned ruefully.

" It looks like a mighty good thing you happened along, though."

After a pause, he added, with a touch of the old resentment.

" I wish I'd made a clean break of it, nevertheless."

He walked to the cave entrance, and stood quietly looking over the moon-sublimated acreage of blackened tree stumps opposite.

" You're after Ben Kynes, of course," he said over his shoulder, a kind of resigned fatalism in his voice.

" I'm after Sergeant Sheridan," Steer corrected gravely. Adding, " And I'm not going back until he's found."

Bradwell's hands had fallen loosely to his side. His breathing was more rapid than usual. Then he said, desperately:

" You're side-stepping the issue. And Ben Kynes didn't mean to kill Jake Perry anyway— it was just a straight fight. Only, Perry fell against some rock."

Steer answered, as gravely as before.

" Ben Kynes *didn't* kill Jake Perry. A fortnight after he'd been shipped to hospital at Prince Albert, Jake was as fit as ever—and with no kick coming at the way Kynes had handled him. Acknowledged the quarrel was his own fault, and that he'd only got what was coming to him!"

Bradwell swung round to him, his face a mask of incredulity.

" But news came down of his death!" he exclaimed breathlessly. " That—that's why Kynes made his getaway!"

" It was not Jake Perry who died," Steer explained, his voice unresponsive to the hope in Bradwell's. " It was his brother Jude. It's quite

understandable why the first report was un-
contradicted. Jake was a stranger to this district,
anyway, and being offered a decent job in the
Porcupines, he simply pulled out of Prince
Albert without coming back."

For the life of him he could not fathom why
Bradwell's expression had cleared of strain.

" Then," he demanded tensely, " Kynes can—
come back?"

For what seemed a long time, Steer looked at
him without speaking. Then he placed his hand
on the boy's shoulders, and looked searchingly into
his face. He answered slowly:

" Yes—if that's all your stepfather has on his
conscience."

As their glances held, gradually there stole into
Bradwell's eyes a look of bewilderment that, as
the significance of Steer's words struck home,
flashed to sudden anger. He wrenched himself
from Steer's grasp.

" If you've anything against Ben Kynes—oh
yes, he's my stepfather all right, and the best
man walking, at that—don't just hint at it. Say
it out like a man."

Steer's eyes were searching, as he said slowly:

" What has he done with Sergeant Sheridan?"

Bradwell went whiter yet, and would have
spoken, but before he could do so, Steer
added:

" It's only fair to tell you they were seen together as Sheridan was ' bringing him in '."

He had expected to see the fear come back into Bradwell's eyes, but instead he read only a certain contempt.

" I know," he admitted. " By old Tom Holt, the Hudson's Bay factor at Fort Nelson. What of it?"

Steer's face was stern as he spread his hands with a suggestion of impotence.

" That was five months ago," he pointed out. " Since then, you've been taking Ben supplies; it was those that were distributed about the map by *Yootin Wetikoo*." His voice sank. " In the meantime—*what's become of Sheridan?*"

Bradwell retorted, challengingly:

" What do you think's become of him?"

" That's what I'm here to find out," Steer reminded him.

Bradwell looked straight to his front for a moment. Then his eyes turned to Steer, and now they were less challenging, than appraising.

" Apart from anything he's done to Sheridan," he said slowly, " you don't—want—my stepfather?"

" Apart from that," Steer replied levelly, " he's as free as any prospector in the North."

Bradwell did not speak for so long that the assurance might have gone unheard. He returned now to his old position against the cliff face, and though his eyes were fixed on the mainland, it was apparent he was taking in but little of what they rested on. At last he said, over his shoulder.

" Any chance of salving some of that truck I was toteing, do you think?"

" With daylight, and a little luck, we should retrieve pretty well all of it," Steer replied gravely —and waited.

" Then, as soon as it's together," Bradwell said surprisingly, " we'd better get down to Puffin's Creek before the fight starts."

" Fight?" Steer's voice was puzzled, and Bradwell nodded. Antagonism forgotten, his expression was faintly ironic.

Then it was that in turn he placed his hands on the policeman's shoulders; swung him round.

" Listen," he said. " Here's the way of it. When Sheridan came up with him, there was something of a free-for-all scrap before my step-father could be persuaded to go along. Then, a week later, and with The Barrens behind them, Sheridan slipped and broke his leg. As it looked like being a pretty bad job, the only thing was to free my stepfather from his irons, so's he could build a cabin.

" A month later, just as his leg was mending nicely, Sheridan took sick—pneumonia, I guess; so Kynes had to set to and nurse him afresh.

Last time I saw them the leg was pretty well as good as new, and though he was still weak as a sick kid, he'd turned the corner."

He hesitated, and then faced Steer defiantly.

" Only, not knowing Perry wasn't dead, my stepfather told Sheridan from the start that if he aimed to take him along when he hit the trail again, there'd be all kinds of trouble."

Though in his experience of the North a situation where the captive has nursed the captor, only to join issue again when the time came for rearrest, was not unprecedented, the Mounted Policeman never had ceased to wonder at a loyalty to code that was proof even against the threat of imprisonment or, as in this case, the shadow of the scaffold itself. With the law unable to follow, how easy to slip away!

" How did you come to get in touch with them?" he asked quietly at last.

" Me?" The lift of Bradwell's brows was genuine surprise. " I call Ben Kynes my step-father, and by blood that's all he is," he explained. " But if he'd been my own father ten times over he couldn't have——"

Reticence intercepting, he broke off.

" Anyway, he means a whole lot to me," he supplemented, after a pause, " and soon as he'd left Lurgan's Landing—why, I just set out to find him. And I found both of 'em."

Above the tree tops that backed the path of the Devil Wind the night sky was paling to the first pearl of dawn. Eastward, the Morning Star glowed like a suspended lamp. A dawn breeze, smoke-laden, ruffled the lake surface, and, dying, left it motionless. Far to the left a loon broke into the stillness.

And as Steer did not speak, in a little while Bradwell said:

" So, after we've collected the stores, I guess we'd best hit the trail—together."

CHAPTER IX

Corporal Steer investigates a "Snatch Racket"

On his way back from his longest patrol of the year, not only was Larry a physically exhausted man, but a very anxious one.

Though he had grown both to like and to sympathize with the Indians, he made no pretence of understanding them. No white man ever does, in his experience. Wise in many ways, in others they were just so many children.

Sickness, for example. Whatever might be the matter with them, they went to their own medicine man, who in nineteen cases in twenty wasn't even a good guesser. And when he failed to cure them, they just threw in their hand, and waited to be returned to Store.

That did not matter so much when it was a single case; but it was the very dickens in an epidemic. And now that the dreaded grippe was raging through the reserve like a prairie fire, neither the chief nor anyone else was doing a thing about it. Further, with so many of the tribe too sick to hunt, they'd blamed little grub, and no medical supplies at all.

Larry had emptied the contents of his first-aid box, and left all his food except enough for the dogs and himself. As bad a business as ever he had come across, and now he was on his way flat out to bring proper help.

About eight o'clock in the evening he saw a light ahead; one whose steadiness told him it came from a cabin window. That looked good to Larry, who after a sixty-odd mile mush since dawn was as nearly all-in as a man may be and remain on his feet. Two or three hours before a stove, with hot coffee, maybe a stew, and the first warm sleep in weeks, and he would be all set for home.

As he drew closer, he saw that the cabin was large and unusually stoutly built; also, that smoke curled from the chimneys. A relief, that—the owner was home; if he had been on his trap-lines, there would have been kindling to cut to replace what he used, for that is the law of the wild. Also, the cabin would have been cold, and he would have had to cook his own grub—if any.

When he *woa-d* his team outside the door, however, to his surprise the owner did not come out to give him welcome.

He rapped at the door, and though he could hear movement inside, there was no response. He

hoped the occupant was not sick; it was bad
enough having those Ojibways thrown on his
hands, without the necessity for detailing a man
as nurse for a trapper.

With the idea of seeing for himself, he seized
the handle. To his astonishment, the door was
locked. Annoyed, now, he rapped hard on it
with the butt of his revolver, replacing the
weapon in its holster, however, at the sound of
footsteps from the other side.

There was the rasp of a turning key; the door
opened by half a dozen inches, and a face looked
out—a broad face, seamed to a thousand creases
by years of sun and frost and wind, and with hard
blue eyes and square, out-thrust jaw. A man,
Larry judged, of about forty-five.

" Well?" demanded the stranger, in a voice
as hard as his eyes.

This was a new one on Larry, and for a moment
he could find nothing to say. In those lonely
places everything the cabin-owner has is placed
ungrudgingly at the service of the wayfarer, and
especially does this apply to the Mounted Police,
who are the friend of all but the wrongdoer.
More often than not, of him as well.

" Aren't you going to ask me inside?" he
blurted at last.

The man was not, and made no bones about
saying so.

" I'll have no Yellerlegs snoopin' around *my* cabin!" he said harshly, using the nickname for the Force, due to the broad stripe of that colour down the uniform breeches.

One of the first lessons the Service teaches is control of the temper. Larry kept his now, but only just.

" When a man doesn't like us around," he said coldly, " nine times in ten it's because he's something to hide."

He saw the man's face change. Not fear, exactly, came into it, so much as a very distinct uneasiness.

" Beat it, Yellerlegs!" he shouted, slammed the door hard in Larry's face, and turned the key.

Larry put in a spell of pretty hard thinking in that long mush to Tamrack. After help had been sent to the reserve, he sought out old Charlie Hall, the woodcutter, an old-timer who knew more of the Yukon than any man in the district.

" Do you know who lives at that cabin at——" Larry gave the map reference of the one where he had received such queer treatment.

The woodcutter nodded.

" Sure," he said. " Old Tom Elsworth. Queer kind of cuss he is, too, since he lost his wife and kid a few years back." He paused,

eyeing Larry curiously. " Hates you fellers like
a cat hates broken glass," he added.

" I'll say he does!" Larry agreed with feeling.
" Only—just *why* does he?"

Charlie's reply came promptly.

" Went to you three or four years ago with a
complaint that Harry Keen had jumped part of
his claim. When you came to go into it, you
found that Harry'd done nothing of the kind;
it was the other way around, as a matter of fact
—Elsworth had squatted part of his. Since
then the only use he's had for the police is to
fling mud at 'em. That's why, when I hear of
you callin' in at his cabin for a brotherly chat,
I want to laugh myself all out of shape!"

Larry thought for a moment. So far as it
went, this was sound enough; the trouble was
that, to his idea, it didn't go far enough.

" Listen, Charlie," he said at last. " Don't
ask me why I'm so darn sure, because I can't
tell you—it's just one of my hunches. But I'll
bet a bright silver dollar to a stale doughnut that
hatred for the Mounted wasn't the only reason
he was so blamed keen to keep me on the far
side of that door!"

The woodcutter shot him a quick keen glance.

" What's back of your mind?" he asked
quickly, but Larry shook his head.

" I've told you," he said. " Just a hunch;

he's something stowed away in that cabin of his that he'd just hate to advertise."

" What *could* he have?" Hall demanded curtly, and Larry gave him the result of considerable thought.

" Being the queer-tempered cuss you describe, what about all he's left of a man after a free-for-all?" he suggested. " Or a pile of furs trapped out of season, and that'd earn him a term ' on the woodpile ' if they were seen? Or a store of raided highgrade?"

Hard-bitten face frowning, the woodcutter thought for a moment.

" None of that sounds like Elsworth to me," he said dubiously at last, and paused. " I don't like the sound of it, nevertheless."

" Maybe I'll apply for a search warrant, and go and have a look-see for myself," Larry suggested, though a shade doubtfully.

The woodcutter snorted.

" Be your age!" he said severely. " What sort of respect do you think folk'd have for the ' Mounted ' if one of their officers went bursting into a citizen's private residence just because he doesn't meet him with a salute of guns an' an address of welcome?"

This was right, and Larry had to let it go at that. And as he was thinking it over, the orderly room door burst open, and an Ojibway from the

5   (F 649)

reserve stalked in. As he stood before the desk, his eye was smouldering; the gaunt frame tense.

"What's the best news from you, Lonely Loon?" Larry inquired equably after a swift glance at him.

"White man—the Flat-mouthed One," the Ojibway said from between set teeth. "Um take Light Footsteps, my papoose, to um cabin. When I say bring um back to Reserve, him pull a gun on me."

The woodcutter glanced meaningly at Larry.

"There you are!" he said confidently. "*That's* what the old man's got in his cabin. Though *why* he should want to kidnap an Indian kid needs one awful lot of explaining."

He turned to the Ojibway.

"Is Light Footsteps the *only* papoose he's taken?" he demanded.

The Indian shook his head.

"No. Him take um——" Of the hands he held up, only the thumbs were not extended.

"Eight!" Larry broke in, his tone startled. "*When* did he take 'em?"

This time the thumbs were added to the fingers.

"Ten days ago, eh?" Larry said thoughtfully. "Well, we all have our hobbies—but I'd rather that old moron was shut up with eight Indian kids than I was."

He nodded at the Ojibway. "Very good, Lonely Loon; I'll attend to it."

The Indian stalked out. By the time the door had closed on him, Larry was at the telephone. When he was through to Division, he told his story to the superintendent.

"Search that cabin right away," 'Old Man' Rivers ordered promptly. "I'll send you the warrant by the next stage, and in the meantime I'll take full responsibility."

"Not that in the ordinary way there's any fear of old Tom harming the kids, or any person else," Charlie Hall observed reflectively, as Larry was harnessing the dog-team. "The danger is, he may have gone 'bush crazy'. And just in case, I guess I'd better come along with you."

With the knowledge of how frequently that isolation-induced scourge manifests itself in an insane hatred of one's fellows, the two mushed at record-breaking pace. It was on a steel-cold mid-morning when, at last, the cabin came in sight, the feather of smoke curling to the sheet-lead sky showing that the prospector was at home. There was no indication that their approach had been observed, nor was there any reply when they knocked at the door.

"Open up there, Elsworth!" Larry shouted at last. "This is an official visit—in the name of the Law!"

At that, after a pause, the door opened, but with the bow-legged, aggressive figure of the claim-holder blocking an entrance through which came the ominous smell of carbolic disinfectant. The coarse-grained face was less apprehensive, Larry observed with interest, than it was furious with anger.

" What's it you're after?" the old man demanded fiercely, but in a tone so low that, involuntarily, Larry hushed his own.

" To have a look-see what it is you're hiding," he said levelly. " There's a search-warrant on the way, but in the meantime I'm coming right in."

The old man stared at him without speaking for a moment. Then:

" That'll be Lonely Loon's doin'," he said slowly. " I got his kid, Light Footsteps, here— among others; an' Lonely Loon kicked like a steer because I wouldn't give him money when I went to fetch him."

He moved away, leaving them to pass inside.

" Step quiet!" he instructed in a low voice.

They " stepped quiet " into the warmth and cleanliness of that bare, dimly lighted cabin; they stood silent only because they could find nothing adequate to say.

On either side of the room were four Hudson Bay blanket-covered spruce-and-chicken-wire

beds. In each, washed, full-fed, in more than one
instance sleeping, and convalescent to a man,
was an Ojibway papoose. Actually, the place
was less a living-room than a hospital ward.

" They'd all a' died—stuck among all the
filth of the reserve," old Tom grumbled. " An'
since I lost that one o' my own—why, I just
can't see a kid suffer without wantin' to help!"

CHAPTER X

Corporal Steer loses his Team

As he reached the lake side, Jerry Parsons checked suddenly in his stride; from behind a tree trunk watched himself being robbed, and his mouth set in a hard line.

Here was confirmation of his suspicions; the reason why after more than a month of the hardest work in years, on the richest trapping-ground in his experience, the result had been so poor.

Jake Skinner, that desert-rat from the prairie provinces, was raiding the traps.

Deliberately, ominously, Jerry stood up; strode over to confront the one who, a fine specimen of marten in his hand, and a rich assortment of pelts on the sledge by his side, wilted visibly at sight of him.

For a matter of seconds the two faced each other without speaking. Then, with a lightning movement of his free hand, Jake had his gun out.

" Stand back, Big Boy!" he snarled, yellow teeth bared, and the reddened eyes in his narrow face gleaming, so that he reminded the trapper of nothing so much as a cornered rat. And, if current rumour went for anything, he was as dangerous.

The only firearm Jerry toted was his rifle, that, slung across his back, was quite un-get-at-able.

" Put up that gun, Skinner," he said levelly, but with little or no hope that the other would obey.

Skinner's thick lips creased to a smile it did Jerry no good to see.

" I gotta hand it to you, fella," he jeered. " You sure know a trapline when you see it— I've collected more pelts from it than you'd find in a Hudson's Bay store."

Keeping his enemy covered, he paused—thinking, apparently, of how this unexpected situation might be turned to advantage. Suddenly an expression of evil overspread the narrow, coarse-grained face.

" Listen, fella," he said harshly. " Up to now I bin aimin' just to empty your traps half a day or so before you turned up; to-day you arrived early, and that's just too bad for you. However, you won't be the first trapper not to ' come in ' at the end of the season, anyway, an' you've only yourself to blame. Put your hands over your head, an' keep 'em there."

Jerry knew better than to deceive himself;

the gleam in Jake's eyes told him that this was no bluff. Either Jerry did as he was ordered, or Jake would shoot.

As the trapper's hands went up, Jake circled until he was at Jerry's back. Then he dug the pistol half an inch into Jerry's spine, made him lower his arms, and slipped a loop of caribou thong about his wrists.

He jerked the dogs to their feet and gathered up the reins.

"Move!" he ordered harshly, and again there was nothing for it but to obey. "Up the main trail half a mile, then left. Hit that trail, and keep on it."

"What about my team?" demanded Jerry, concerned for those five spike-eared malemutes of his own breeding that were the pride of his life.

"Guess the wolves'll attend to them, all right," Skinner snarled callously, and if ever Jerry had known hate it was at that moment. In common with all good mushers, his dogs were his first consideration.

Five miles away, concealed in the thickest of the scrub, was Skinner's cabin—canvas slung over a framework erected over a two-foot high foundation of logs. Here, stretched on frames, or packed into bales, was a harvest of furs that would have made any Hudson's Bay factor's mouth water. Inside, Jake bound his prisoner's ankles and thrust him into a roughly-made chair.

" Stay put—while I boil coffee," he grunted, and, to his victim's surprise, produced not one cup, but two.

When the stove was lighted and the coffee bubbling in the pot, Jake's hand went to the inner pocket of his parka; fumbled there for a moment. As he withdrew his hands, Jerry saw a small object fall to the floor, where, half concealed in the accumulated dust, it lay unnoticed by Jake Skinner.

" Guess you can do with this, anyway," Jake said at last, holding a fragrant-smelling cup to Jerry's lips.

Jerry drank.

A moment later the walls of the cabin seemed to quiver, sway forward, and close in on him. Everything went black, and he knew no more. . . .

When he came to himself, it was a little before he remembered where he was. Gradually, however, recollection came, and to his astonishment he found that his hands and feet were free, and that there was no sign of Skinner, nor of the object that had dropped from his pocket. He must have noticed it lying there and picked it up, Jerry concluded, and he hoped fervently that was the case.

But there was nothing left of the harvest of

furs; nor, when Jerry went outside, of the sledge or dog-team.

What, he asked himself, was Jake's idea in leaving him free to report his loss to the Mounted Police? Actually, the more thought Jerry gave to the situation, the less sense he was able to make of it.

However, there it was, and it was up to him to beat it while the going was good. Even with the loss of his team, he could be at his own camp in a matter of hours. Once there, he'd load a hand toboggan with grub, and set out for the police barracks straight away.

To his further astonishment, approaching the place where he had left his team, he was greeted by the low whimper of Snowball, the leader. Around the next turn in the trail, moreover, there was the whole outfit, complete with the grub he had brought for his four-days' tour of the traplines.

Unspeakably cheered, though still wondering, Jerry set off. When he reached his camp, the mystery was disclosed in one blinding flash of illumination.

Instead of the stoutly-built, comfortably equipped cabin, where had been stored his kit and what few furs he had collected since the beginning of the season, there was only a smouldering ruin.

It did not need the trail of sledge-runners and snowshoes to tell him who was responsible for the fire, nor of the motive behind it. With fiendish forethought, Jake had revived the old cruel trick that in the old bad days the " free-traders " of the North-West Company used to spring on their rivals of Hudson's Bay.

His cabin gutted, Jerry was left, without supplies, to perish in the wilderness.

The fiendish cunning of it! For whereas his own unwounded body lying beside the sledge some distance from a burnt-out cabin would be put down only to the luck of the trail, a corpse, discovered starved to death and with bound hands and feet, would tell unmistakably of murder.

Besides, since that spring, the Mounted Police had shown a marked curiosity as to Jake's where-abouts and activities at the time of the disappear-ance of one Ike Peters, whose bullet-riddled body had been found at the foot of Maple Falls.

Ike had spent the winter squandering the gold that, during the summer, he had picked from the one highgrade seam that ran through the low-grade of his claim. With nothing but a worn-out tobacco pouch on the body, and not a trace of the gold elsewhere, it was obvious that robbery had been the motive for the crime. . . .

Anxiously Jerry went through his supplies on

the sledge.   Apart from matches, emergency fuel, a first-aid set, and a box of spare cartridges, there was grub for a normal four days for man and team.   With severe rationing, say eight for himself, and six for the malemutes.   It would not do to weaken the team, for with the dogs lay his only hope of survival. . . .

Tamrack, the nearest settlement, was more than six hundred miles away—even with the dogs full-fed, about a fortnight's mush.   The only chance was that he might meet another team on the trail.

Nevertheless, as he was not going to throw in his hand without a fight, he set off straight away, and made a good ten miles before, after a bite of bacon and bannock for himself and a couple of dried jackfish for the team, he crawled into his sleeping-bag.

Following the main trail all the next morning, he made good time.   And then, about noon, he saw another trail branching off between the trees.

Suddenly, breathlessly, he halted and went back.   Something noticed from the tail of his eye as he swept past had struck a note of familiarity.

His heart took a bound of elation at what he saw.   If there was nothing individual about the marks of the sledge-runners, this did not apply to those made by the snowshoes. The print showed clearly where the webbing had been repaired, and because it was so clumsily executed, Jerry had particularly noticed an exactly corresponding defect in the shoes Skinner had kicked off in his camp.

Reviewing the situation, it was some little time before Jerry made a move. This new trail led, not to Tamrack, but away from it.

For where, then, was Jake bound?

Then, quite suddenly, Jerry had a hunch, startling, but if it was correct, infinitely revealing. Continued, the new trail would lead directly to the Alaskan border—to American territory. And from Skagway, a fugitive could take ship to Seattle, and from there disappear into the blue. Even if he was traced, which was extremely doubtful, United States extradition law being what it is, he would take a lot of getting back to Canadian soil.

Well, if Jerry could help it, Jake wasn't going to get out of Canada. Though, with next to no grub, and only five dogs to the other's seven, he himself might be dead of starvation before he came within twenty miles of his quarry, it was up to him to camp on the trail of one who, now, he was convinced, not only was a poacher, but a murderer, and a particularly brutal one at that.

He gave an anxious look to his team and, to

an extent, was reassured by what he saw. Tails curled stifly over their backs, spike ears sharply erect, the dogs were in their usual good shape. He found himself wondering rather bleakly for how long that well-being would continue.

Nursing the team as best he could, resting only long enough to conserve their strength, he pushed forward and ever forward, with Skinner's trail clear before him. And the more ground he covered, the more certain it became that this forlorn hope was doomed to the final disaster.

Grub, of course, was the problem; in the thin and rarefied atmosphere of 40 below zero, both man and beast required constant re-fueling to keep going, and with not even a jack-rabbit in the way of game, his own " fuel " was shrinking dismally. Soon, all the supplies he had left for himself was a handful of flour, an ounce or two of lard, and a pinch of tea and sugar; for the dogs, only one small jackfish.

Then came the night when, with man and beast still ravenous, there was nothing left at all.

Well, he told himself, here was the end; just one of those things that happen to a man in the rich but merciless north.

The irony of it was, too, that if only he could have made the grade, he would have caught up with his quarry; every indication told him he was gaining hand over fist; more than once the ashes of Skinner's last camp-fire had been still warm.

At the end of the seventh day, half-starved for a week, and wholly starved for thirty-six hours, the team petered out; tails lankly trailing, ears flat to the head, eyes dulled and staring, legs uncertain.

In the night, awakened by whimpering, Jerry discovered Oki, the oldest and weakest malemute in the team, at the last extremity.

So he took her into the wood out of sight of the others, shot and skinned her; cooked the carcass, and fed it to the dogs. They devoured it ravenously, and in the morning were strong enough for the trail again.

And that was more than Jerry was; for two days he had lived on half a can of condensed milk and the carcass of a whisky-jack—a bird about the size of a magpie—that he had found dead beneath a tree.

By midday, he realized he had reached his limit. Two toes were frozen through lack of warming food; his legs as indiarubber beneath him, so that, mushing behind the team, he staggered like a drunken man.

Then, in the early afternoon, the last phase set in—the " Madness of the Woods ", as the Indians call it. The trees between which he passed became alive; advancing and receding;

faces, grinning and mouthing, danced and quivered before his eyes; gigantic forms, misshapen and grotesque, stalked or pranced across the avenues ahead.

Without warning, at the moment when Jerry thought his legs were doubling beneath him for the last time, Snowball dug her forefeet so stubbornly in the trail that the other dogs piled about her. From that anchorage, whining excitedly, dropping tail waving, questing nostrils aquiver, no persuasion could induce her to move.

Dimly Jerry wondered what had seized her; what it was she had scented. Not wolves; in that case she would be all out for pushing on. Not caribou; this wasn't caribou country, and he would have heard them.

He looked about to discover what was in the wind.

It was not until his eyes travelled upward that, his heart rocketing into his throat, he saw what already the malemute had scented.

Just ahead, and slightly to the left, four spruce trees formed the corners of a ten-foot square. Lashed to this, six feet or so above Jerry's head, was a tarpaulin-covered platform.

He breathed a fervent prayer of gratitude to the Mounted Police who, in what long experience tells them are the most suitable places, establish these animal-proof caches of food, that, except in case of direst necessity, it is one of the most serious crimes in the north to rifle.

Painfully, by reason of his weakness, he climbed the most negotiable of those living corner-posts; helped himself reasonably to all he needed for himself and his team; carefully refastened the cases; left a note to say what he had taken, and replaced the tarpaulin.

After he had cooked the first nourishing meal he had eaten in days, and fed the clamouring team, he turned in by the fire for the sleep that would restore him to something of his old enduring self. The loss of time couldn't be helped; he'd do his best to make up for it later.

He awakened to bright moonlight and a touch on his shoulder. Starting up, he saw that a figure was bending over him, slim, purposeful, his parka gay with the multi-coloured ribbons that are a guard against the dreaded snow-blindness. And on the collar, the buffalo-head badge of the Royal Canadian Mounted Police.

" Well, for crying in the soup!" cried Jerry in astonishment, " if it isn't Larry Steer!"

" In the flesh, old-timer," the policeman replied equably. " And though you're the last man I could've hoped to come across right in mid-season hundreds of miles from your trap-line, I'll say you're welcome, all right. So would anyone be who had a dog-team."

Jerry jerked upright in his sleeping-bag.

" For the love of Pete, you don't mean you set out from Tamrack without a team?" he exclaimed.

The policeman shook his head.

" I'll say I didn't. I wish I had. Then I shouldn't have lost seven of the best huskies in the Territory, a new Indian-made hickory-wood sledge, a month's rations, and all my gear, through thin ice on Tidal river," he said bitterly.

Jerry made sympathetic noises.

" Tough luck!" he said, and meant it. " Pity you hadn't my old Snowball as leader. With thin ice ahead, no dog-musher living could keep her on a straight course. . . . Guess you had to make here to raid your own cache," he added, and Larry nodded.

" And found you'd been here before me," he agreed. " What are you doing in this neck-of-the-woods, anyway?"

" Chasing a murderer," Jerry replied, and saw how the officer stiffened.

" How come?" he demanded quietly. " That sort of thing's more up my street than yours, anyway. Who's the killer, and who did he kill?"

" Jake Skinner," replied Jerry, " murdered Ike Peters. Not that that'll surprise you a whole lot, if I know anything," he added.

If the corporal was surprised, he refrained from showing it.

"What makes you so sure?" he asked, and Jerry did not hesitate.

"Do you remember that nugget Ike used always to tote around with him?" he demanded. "The first piece of gold ever he took from his claim. Shaped like a baby's hand holding a little doll."

The other nodded.

"Sure," he confirmed. "It was his mascot; wouldn't have parted with it for a thousand dollars. What about it?"

"I caught Jake raiding my traplines," Jerry said levelly. "When I went up to ask him what the heck, he pulled a gun on me, and forced me into his camp. When he took a bottle of knock-out drops from his pocket to put me to sleep, Ike's nugget dropped on the floor. When I came out of the ether, both Jake and the nugget had gone. So I guess he'll have it with him right now."

"And so you came right after him?" Larry suggested.

"Since he'd burnt down my cabin and everything in it, I'd 've followed him from Hades to a week on Tuesday," Jerry stated with emphasis.

"Where's he headin' for, anyway?" the policeman asked.

" Alaska, if I know anything," said Jerry.
" And once he crosses the border—good-bye-e-e!"

" How far do you figure you're behind him?"
the policeman asked quickly.

" From eight to twelve hours, I guess," the
trapper hazarded, and Larry shot a keen scrut-
inizing glance at the team, curled muzzle to stern
in the snow.

" Malemutes in good shape?" he demanded.

" Sure—now they're full-fed," the trapper
replied confidently.

" Then, if you're rested up, we'll pull out
right away, Larry said decisively. " And I'll
say we'll have to go some to catch up before
Skinner reaches the border."

" I'll say we will," Jerry agreed. " Especially
as I had to shoot one of my dogs, and Skinner
has seven. But as he'll have no notion there's
anyone camping on his trail, maybe he won't
hurry," he added hopefully.

" What like are his dogs?" the constable
inquired, and Jerry shrugged his shoulders.

" Good enough—if only he knew how to
mush 'em," he said with the contempt of the
northern trailsman for a " desert-rat " from the
Prairie Provinces. " His only notion of getting
'em to work is by lashin' 'em, an' you know what
a huskie's reaction is to that. He'll pull just as
hard as he has to, and not a half-ounce harder."

Three days later, when they broke camp at dawn, the temperature had risen perceptibly from that of the day before. After an hour's hard mushing, Jerry, pausing, sniffed at the heightening breeze.

" I don't like the signs," he said quietly, with a glance at a sky that was banking sullenly with cloud.

" Nor do I," Larry agreed. " Heading for blizzard, if I know anything."

Thinking, the trapper did not speak for a moment. Then he laughed shortly.

" If it's awkward for us, what's it going to be for the desert-rat we're chasing?" he said at last.

" We shall make up quite a lot of time—if the snow doesn't blot out his trail altogether," the corporal agreed doubtfully, and Jerry urged the dogs to an increased pace.

Soon, as they had expected, the wind began rising steadily, and the first snowflakes of the coming storm drifted across the landscape. Then, for a quarter of an hour or so, as the day grew grimly darker, there was an ominous lull.

With devastating suddenness, the blizzard broke. Out of the darkness, the hurricane wind, that at times halted man and dogs as surely as a brick wall, drove the snow into their faces with the force of small-shot, robbing them of breath.

This was one of the many occasions when Jerry was rewarded for his long, expert, and kindly training of his dogs. Buffeted, blinded, exhausted by the force of the tempest, they had no thought of quitting; just so long as their master decided to forge ahead, they were with him to the last half-ounce of endurance.

The corporal edged up to Jerry, shouted in his ear above the tumult.

"I've been in this country before," he announced. "By my reckoning, we're not above a mile or two from Cranberry Lake. There's a deserted cabin at the edge, and if we stick to this trail, I believe we'll strike it. If so, we'll rest for an hour and cook some grub."

In one way, actually, they were luckier than they had reason to expect. In a lull in the storm, an hour or so later, when for a few moments a temporary break in the clouds made visibility of a sort, the dark bulk of the cabin loomed uncertainly ahead, with, a hundred or so yards farther on, the snow-covered surface of the lake.

What they failed to notice, however, was the vicious, fear-ridden figure crouched under cover of the cabin's farther side. Jake Skinner, when he had gone to harness up at daybreak, had found no dogs to harness. As happens not infrequently to the consistently brutal musher, the dogs had chosen the hazard of the forest rather than the unceasing brutality of the trail.

Ever since then, his sledge cached out of sight, Jake had been lurking in the hut, despairingly trying to figure how he was to reach the Alaskan border, that was still nearly two hundred miles away.

Then, suddenly, from outside, he had heard the cries of men encouraging a team; dashing frenziedly to the window, had recognized the man he feared most on earth—Corporal Larry Steer—the man who, quietly, grimly, and persistently, had been dogging his footsteps ever since the discovery of Ike Peter's body in the spring—hoping and searching for the final proof that would convince a jury.

Trembling with terror, Jake slipped out of the door that faced the lake. . . .

"No good going on until the storm lets up," Larry remarked, *woa-ing* the team. "Any ground we covered in a blizzard like this would be lost twenty times over by what it took out of us to make it. By the time there was clear going again, we'd be too all-in to move."

"In that case," Jerry said, speaking from the heart, "let's hope Skinner keeps on keeping on. . . . I'll take the team around the end of the cabin, where the dogs'll be in some kind of shelter."

At these words the fugitive's heart almost stopped its beat; only, after a second or so, to pound furiously in his throat.

But there was no need for panic. He heard the door slam open as the corporal entered the hut; was conscious of movement as the team skirted the side; of the trapper unloading the grub-box and the makings of a meal from the sleigh. Then he heard the hut door slam shut as Jerry joined the policeman inside. . . .

"Good!" the trapper exclaimed, glancing about the bare, roughly-furnished room. "Stove in pretty good shape, as well—and with a heap of kindling in the corner."

"And the stove still alight," Larry pointed out. "So we're not far behind."

Snowshoes discarded, their moccasined feet were silent as they moved about the room. Suddenly, sounds reached them from the outside.

"For the love of *Mike*!" shouted Larry, and with Jerry at his heels, dashed for the door.

They were too late! Already more than fifty yards down the lakeside slope, and urged by the furious lashing of the unaccustomed caribou-thong from the driver who mushed them, the malemutes were making a speed that no man on snowshoes could approach.

"And with the nearest cabin close on two hundred miles to the north, I'll say Skinner's put one over us for fair—and I don't mean maybe," Larry observed grimly.

If Jerry did not immediately reply, it was due only to physical inability, for at that instant the blizzard swept up with a fury that, beating full into his face with a force that made anything that had gone before seem like a summer zephyr in comparison, hurled the words chokingly back into his throat.

And as, seizing the corporal by the arm, he pulled him back into the hut, darkness closed down again as suddenly as if all light had been switched off at the main.

" I'll say we're sunk with all hands, all right." Larry said with finality, throwing himself into a chair.

" Don't you believe it!" Jerry said confidently.

Eyes alert, Larry looked up sharply.

" What in Sam Hill do you mean?" he jerked.

" You'll see—in a half to three-quarters of an hour's time," the trapper replied. " Meantime, what about some eats?"

During the meal, when the storm outside raged with a fury beyond the experience of either, no cross-examination by the corporal could induce Jerry to explain. By the time the plates were washed, however, the sky had lightened enough to enable them to distinguish the lake shore.

At last, turning from the window where he had taken station a quarter of an hour before:

" Slip into your parka and snowshoes," Jerry instructed quietly, reaching for his own as he spoke.

Puzzled, Larry followed his companion to the beach. And there, dimly, across the lake, he was able to make out a darker blur against the snow; a blur, moreover, that was moving in towards them.

To his amazement he saw, a few minutes later, that it was Jerry's team—and Jake Skinner.

The sledge reached the bank; led by the panting, tongue-lolling leader, toiled up the slope.

Grim-faced, Larry stepped forward; touched the murderer on the shoulder as regulations demand.

" I arrest you, Jacob Skinner," he began formally—and stopped.

" For the love of Mike," he cried, turning to the trapper, " if he isn't asleep!"

Jerry nodded.

" Haven't you heard of *Torngek*, the Indian's Evil Spirit of the Storm, who lures men to sleep in blizzard, so that, frozen to death, they never awaken?" he demanded. " That's what's got Skinner—what every dog-musher who knows his business fights as he fights nothing else on earth. It was what I was banking on—partly."

They hauled Skinner, grey-faced and cringing, from the sledge, and to his feet. When, after the formal arrest, Larry went through his prisoner's clothing, in an inner pocket of his parka was the baby's hand nugget that had belonged to the murdered Ike Peters.

Confronted with that evidence, frozen, and without food since the night before, Skinner's spirit broke.

"I killed Peters, all right," he muttered sullenly. "For his gold; you'll find it parked in the sledge I've hid in the scrub. . . ."

Larry was unusually quiet as they thawed out and fed the prisoner.

"What's eating you?" Jerry demanded at last, when the murderer was settled for the night.

"You said that Skinner falling asleep was *partly* what you were banking on," Larry questioned. "What was the other part, anyway?"

Jerry laughed.

"Snowball," he explained. "If that malemute has a fault, it's that in a blizzard there's no musher on earth can stop her going in circles —so that always she comes back to where she started!"

CHAPTER XI

Corporal Steer investigates the Sinister

It was in the father and mother of a temper that Larry made camp that night. He had been chasing Big Bill Hanson through the scrub for two whole days, and seemed about as likely to catch up with him now as before he started. Just at his busiest time, too, when all the half-yearly returns were due to be sent to Dawson.

It wasn't as if the crime for which he was gunning after Big Bill was anything particularly serious. Bill wasn't a "bad man," or anything approaching it; there was no real harm in him at all. He was merely a bad lad, who had beaten up Jim McCoy, the storekeeper, and to evade the inevitable fourteen days in the tie-up, had made for the wide spaces.

And what Big Bill didn't know about the wide spaces, the most difficult routes through, and the speediest method of negotiating them, simply wasn't knowledge. So that, no mean trailsman himself, Larry had to confess himself beaten all along the line—horse, foot, and guns.

Such circumstances not making for good temper, the constable promised himself bitterly that, once he had the fugitive safely in the cooler, he would bring all his influence to bear to see that, instead of the usual fortnight, the portable steel cell in the space in the rear of the orderly room should be occupied for a full twenty-eight days.

Larry's temper had not improved when, awakened at the first streak of dawn, after a hasty cup of coffee, he pushed forward—if he couldn't compete on level terms with his quarry for speed, the only thing was to travel longer hours.

In that morning of heat and brilliant sunshine, his pack as if filled with lead about his shoulders, he had made about ten miles when, emerging from the forest-belt into a flat, level, and, for that area, barren and rock-strewn clearing, he jerked to a halt.

For at the far side of the clearing was a cabin —one that bore the appearance of having been left for a long time unoccupied.

And as, motionless, he stood within the shadow of the trees, slowly at first, and then quite definitely, a memory, a little uncertain, but uneasy, began to stir. Though to the best of his recollection this was the first time he had set eyes on it, there was something about that cabin that wasn't *right*.

He unhitched his pack and, taking the map
that, with an elaborate commentary at the back,
had been so carefully prepared by Constable
Walls, his predecessor at Tamrack, he traced
his route from the barracks.

Yes, there the cabin was, plainly marked;
immediately above, in red, the figure 9.

He turned the map over and read:

" 9. Known as Sinister Shack. Built originally
in 1911 by Tom Forrester, the trapper, who
prospected from there in the summer. Found
dead in his bunk, for no ascertainable cause, in
July, 1912. Cabin taken over by Jim Banks in
the winter of same year. Found dead in his
bunk, in June, 1913. Shack unoccupied until
late 1916, when, owing to high price of furs due
to the war, it was acquired by Charlie Bennett.
Found dead in bunk in July, 1917. Has been
regarded since as a good place to keep away
from."

So *that* was it. Though those tragic events had
happened so long ago as to have been pretty
well forgotten, Larry remembered now, clearly
enough. In any case it was more than probable
that the sequence of deaths had been simply
coincidence—men who, worn out with the hard-
ships of life in the north, had passed away in
their sleep. So far as he had been told, all three
were men long past their prime.

Meantime, too, this wasn't getting on with the job of corralling Big Bill Hanson. And what more probable place for the old nuisance to pass the night than a perfectly good shack? But as, given advance warning, it was fairly certain there'd be a pretty big scrap before Larry could slip the irons on him, in the hope of catching the weasel asleep it would be as well to make his approach as silently as possible.

So he made no sound as he passed across the rock-paved, boulder-strewn clearing; nor when he tried the door.

Handle in hand, he listened intently, but no sound came from within. Noiselessly, then, he turned the handle, swung the door open inch by cautious inch, and, soft-footed, entered.

The window curtains were drawn, so that, except for the shaft of sunlight from the open door, the interior was in semi-darkness. Peering intently about him, Larry could distinguish only faintly the various articles the room contained; table, a couple of chairs, stove—and, against the wall in the far corner, the dark blur of a bunk. But no sign of Big Bill.

He went quietly over to the window that immediately faced the bunk; drew the curtain so that the light would fall on it. And at what that shaft of sunshine disclosed, his heart beating jig-time, in one bound he had crossed the floor and was bending over the still figure of the man who lay there.

Face a sickly leaden colour, eyes closed, thick lips puffed unnaturally outward, it would have taken more noise than an ordinary unrestricted arrival to awaken Big Bill Hanson at that moment. If the old ruffian was breathing at all, there was no indication of it.

Larry lifted the inert body from the bunk, and, so that he would have more room, light, and air, laid it outside the door. There was no pulse that he could feel, and pressing his ear to Big Bill's chest, he could detect no sign of heart-beat. But when he put the corner of his shaving mirror between those protruding lips, he found on it the slightest indication of mist.

Thereafter, he was busy with the first-aid at which every Royal Canadian Mounted Policeman is an adept. Slowly, gradually, but, he was grateful to see, cumulatively, the signs of revival increased; the breathing, heart-beat, and pulse, became more perceptible; then the huge frame stirred uneasily. An hour of hard work in an atmosphere that brought the perspiration running in tiny rivulets down Larry's body, and Big Bill was sitting up and looking dazedly about him.

" What in Sam Hill's happened?" he grunted at last. He peered uncertainly into Larry's face. " You're Yellerlegs Steer, aintcha?"

" *Corporal* Steer to you," Larry corrected, more relieved at having snatched the old ruffian from death than he had any intention of showing. " And as to what's happened, it's for you to tell *me*."

Heavy brows knitted, Big Bill seemed to reflect for a moment.

" You've got *me* beat!" he said rather desperately at last. " All I know is that when I got to here last night, after that two days' song-an'-dance through the scrub, I was about all in, so that there bunk looked pretty good. As I meant to be up an' on my way bright an' early, I turned in to shut-eye straight away. . . .

" Next thing I knew I wuz with my head feelin' as if someone'd filled it with decayed lead, an' my mouth an' throat like I dunno what, and I wuz bein' made a pudden of. When I prized my eyes open, there wuz you doin' your first-aid stuff. . . . And I guess," the patient added after a pause, " that if you hadn't of been right slick an' clever, I should've passed right out to the Happy Huntin' Grounds by this. . . . Queer that—you settin' off after a feller to take him to the tie-up, an' endin' by savin' his life. I guess I got to say ' thank you '!"

Larry looked hard at him, and was reassured by what he saw. Already the leaden tint had dispersed from the coarse-grained face in favour of a more healthy colour, and the eyes were more alert.

" Don't let any question of thanks worry you," he said practically. " I'd always sooner have a live prisoner than a dead one, anyway. . . . Anything been matter with your heart lately? Fainting, or anything like that?"

Sitting up in his blankets, Big Bill snorted indignantly.

" Faintin', nothing!" he declared with emphasis. " My heart's as sound as yours. And so's all the rest of me."

If the huge muscular frame, or the life the big man lived from day to day, was anything to go by, this was nothing but the truth. Yet the astonishing fact remained that having fallen asleep an apparently healthy man, he had awakened only as the result of well over an hour's artificial respiration. The two conditions simply didn't make sense. . . . Unless, of course, in the remote event of there being something harmful about the shack—where already three men had suffered sudden and wholly unexpected death.

Sceptical as Larry was of this solution, when, turning back into the room, he looked on that age-rotted furniture, the cobweb-ridden corners, and red-rusted stove, he had to agree with Constable Walls that, indeed, it was a good place to keep away from.

Then it came to him that to keep away was just one of those things that simply are not done. In other words, if by chance there was dirty work at the cross-roads, then, as a policeman, the cross-roads was the very place where he should be found. Another thing—far recovered as Big Bill was, it would be a good twenty-four hours before he would be fit for the trail.

" Rest here 'til the morning, anyway," he said as he helped that still-bemused man into the cabin and to a chair.

Big Bill nodded.

" Good!" he said with satisfaction. Then his face clouded. " But if you think I'm a-goin' to sleep on that there bunk, you've another guess comin'. Once is too much for me, and if I never see it again, that'll be too soon an' often."

Larry regarded him with a greater surprise than, actually, he felt.

" If you think the bunk's anything to do with you passing out," he said, " we'll run the rule over it right now."

There and then he stripped off the blankets. And when this was done, there was practically nothing left to examine—just a frame cut from the branches of a beech tree, covered with chicken-wire, and nailed on to four legs of a similar wood; beneath, the bare rock upon which the hut was built.

There was a box containing rusty tools in the lean-to shed at the back, and with a gimlet from that store, Larry drilled holes here and there in the frame and legs of the bed. But, as he expected, with no result.

"Whatever it was put you out," he said definitely, "had nothing to do with the bunk, anyway."

Big Bill, however, sniffed sceptically.

"Then *you* can sleep on it," he declared resolutely, "because I'm darn' sure I won't."

"If you'll give me your word not to make your getaway in the night," Larry responded, "I'll do just that, and with the little shut-eye I've had the last two-three nights, only too glad of the chance of a decent rest."

"Watch out you don't rest too long," his prisoner observed prophetically, and Larry was glad to let it go at that.

Though with Big Bill's steel-wire constitution swinging closer back to the normal with every hour, they idled the day away quite happily, with the coming of darkness Larry observed that his companion was becoming more and more uneasy.

"Exactly what is it that's eating you, Bill?" he inquired at last, but with a shrewd idea of what would be the answer.

"I don't like you usin' that bunk," the other

replied without hesitation. " Three men died in it already, an' another as near to death as kiss my hand. I just don't *like* it, an' there's no use sayin' I do."

Neither did Larry like it, and even less so as the time advanced for turning in. Indeed, even though what had gone before could be nothing but coincidence, if it had not been that to draw back now would be to lower the prestige of his Service, he would have chosen somewhere else to sleep.

" Forget it!" he said shortly. " Where do you propose to sleep, anyway?"

The reply came immediately.

" Outside the door of this shack," Big Bill said with decision, and on the whole Larry could not bring himself to blame him.

With Big Bill curled up in his blankets on the one soft patch the clearing provided, however, Larry turned in at last, and, his heart beating perhaps a shade more rapidly than usual, lay for a long time staring into the darkness.

Afterwards, he was never able to remember anything between that period of alertness and blank unconsciousness. One moment he seemed to be as awake as ever in his life, the next a cool night wind was blowing across his face, his head felt as if it was filled with a sponge that had been soaked in stagnant water, and Big Bill was pulling his arms backwards and forwards to expand and contract his chest.

Too dazed and uncertain for protest, but with his head gradually clearing and his strength returning, for quite a long time he was content to stay put. At last, however, struggling suddenly free, he spoke.

" I seem to have got it pretty much as you did," he said uncertainly.

Big Bill nodded.

" If I hadn't felt kind of anxious, an' got up to see how you wuz kippin' down," he said soberly, " you'd 've got it worse. I never seen a feller as far gone as what you were that hasn't handed in his pay-sheet. Wait, an' I'll get you a cup of cawfee. That I'll boil on a fire *outside* the shack—thank you very much."

The hot drink went further to revive Larry, and thanks to his well-disciplined habits and sound constitution, by the time the sun showed above the tree-tops, he was much his old self again. Also, he was more than a little angry, and to the last degree, determined.

" Listen, Bill," he said in a hard voice. " It's one of our strictest rules not to make bargains with prisoners, but in your case it's one I'm going to break. Help me find what's wrong with this shack, and we'll forget about what you did to McCoy." He added, resolutely: " But bargain or no bargain, if I have to pull the shack down to find the trouble, I'm not leaving here 'til I've got the whole thing cleared up."

Big Bill glanced at him keenly for a moment before turning away.

"We'll call that a deal," he said shortly; "but I'd've stayed right with you, anyway. With a trapper or prospector liable to drop in for a night at any time, it sure ain't safe to leave the cabin as it is."

Though they spent a couple of hours or more searching for a clue to the mystery, at the end of which time there was no inch of space nor article in or about the shack they had not examined as closely as if through a microscope, it was only to draw a blank.

"Of course," Big Bill remarked, mopping his forehead, "there's plenty of fellers say the joint's haunted—that it's spooks who don't want folks to sleep here."

"And what do you think yourself?" said Larry, knowing how superstitious the loneliness and silence of the North have rendered so many of his fellows.

"That there ain't no such things," the prospector declared sturdily.

"Then where does the trouble lie?" Larry demanded. "Through human agency?"

Big Bill gave one of his emphatic head-shakes.

"Not on your life!" he declared. "What sleep I had last night was so light the littlest sound would've had me jumpin' to my feet like a startled moose. And I'll lay all the money I ever hope to earn there wasn't a man or woman within a hundred miles of us."

"Then what in Sam Hill *is* it?" Larry demanded desperately, and there was one of his characteristic pauses before he spoke again. "But as that seems to be the centre of the trouble, we'll take another look at the bunk—shall we?"

"I've looked at it until my eyes hurt," Big Bill said despondently, "and all I can see is a wooden frame, four legs and a couple of running yards of chicken-wire. Still, if you feel that way about it. . . ."

So they went over, and though there was nothing more than Big Bill had described, Larry remained for so long without moving that Big Bill began to grow impatient.

"What is it you're looking at?" he demanded sarcastically at last.

Unmoved by the tone, Larry pointed a fore-finger at the floor that could be seen so plainly beneath the wire.

"At a crack in the rock—that isn't there," he said slowly, and Big Bill shrugged his shoulders.

"What am I supposed to say now?" he said

unpleasantly. " The higher the fewer, or something?"

Pivoting on his heel, Larry turned to him.

" Don't you remember, when we gave this bunk the once-over early yesterday, that even if it was mighty narrow and less than an inch deep, there was a crack here—under the chicken wire right at the head of the bed?"

Big Bill shook his head.

" I was looking at the bed, not at the ground," he admitted, and Larry grinned.

" You should take a course with our C.I.B.,"[1] he said. " Wait while I show you."

He pulled the bed-frame aside, and with the magnifying-glass that every man in the North carries to examine specimens of quartz for gold specks, made a minute inspection of the rock. Then he handed the glass to Big Bill, and traced an irregular line with the point of his penknife.

" See?" he asked, and Big Bill nodded.

" Sure," he agreed. " But what's it mean, anyway?"

" Wait 'till after sundown," Larry said, and refused further discussion until the heat of the day began to give way to the keen cold air that even in the height of summer comes with nightfall in the North.

" Don't strike a light until I give the word,"

[1] Criminal Investigation Branch.

he instructed as they went over to the bunk. "I've my torch ready."

He shone the beam on the place they had examined in the morning. But instead of an almost undetectable line it had required his knife blade to indicate, now there was a fissure nearly a quarter of an inch wide, and more than a full inch in depth.

"It'll get wider as the rock cools, as well," Larry said warningly. "Keep back a little, and don't breathe more than you have to."

He took a box of matches from his pocket.

"Hold the torch, and watch this, and be thankful that neither of us went out like it," he said quietly.

He struck a match well away from the fissure; when the flame had obtained good hold he brought it forward.

The flame turned blue, sank, and went out.

"But what's it *mean*?" Big Bill cried tensely.

There was no hesitation in the reply.

"Carbon monoxide," Larry told him. "Odourless, colourless—and deadly. When the heat of the sun expands the rock, the gas is sealed up in the earth. When the heat's replaced by cold, the rock contracts—and releases the gas. Like a good many other mysteries, simple as kiss my hand—when you know how it's done."

Big Bill looked at him hard. Here was a

policeman laying down the law like a scientist.

" But how do you *know*?" he demanded.

" Because a policeman's no use in this neck-of-the-woods unless he knows a bit about everything—some that he's taught, and the rest that he learns by experience," Larry said as he went over to the wood fire in the corner, and began shifting the logs one by one to a position close to the outer wall of the cabin.

There were several blocks of solidified paraffin in his pack for use in the tiny folding cooker he used in areas where there was no fuel. And one of these highly inflammable blocks he placed at the base of the bonfire.

" Collect your blankets and gear," he said over his shoulder. " Then hand me that box of matches —and watch!"

CHAPTER XII

Corporal Steer witnesses a Transfer

It had been a long trail from Crawfish, and when Good reached the claim, it came on to rain—one of those unheralded, short-lived storms that are so usual in the Yukon. As it was still half a mile or more to the cabin, he sheltered beneath the trees that fringed the workings.

The rain came down, not in sheets, but in solid rods of water that, rebounding from the bared rock of the claim, lent the illusion of a swiftly-moving tide, and that rattled in the leaves overhead like hail on corrugated zinc.

Presently, one of the branches acting as conduit, a steady stream began to spout on to the moss-covered rock upon which the Englishman was seated, so that he was forced to edge away.

But it was a good half-hour after the storm had died away that, with the sun filtering warmly through the trees to dry out a drenched and glistening world, he passed on to the cabin.

There was no sign of movement from within; and when he opened the door, to his disappointment, the place was empty. There was, however, a sheet of paper pinned to the table.

"*sorry ole timer but I got to pull out to new westminster my old muther is sick plese call agen in about 3 weeks Skagway.*"

Being there by appointment, Good was rather more than disappointed. Though he was sorry enough for Skagway's mother, he wanted to see, and if it was as represented, to buy, the claim. He'd been in the country ever since break-up, and was tired of being pointed at as a cheechako Englishman who couldn't find a job for himself.

As he was cooking his midday meal on the homeward trail next day, Larry Steer caught up with him.

"What you doing in this neck-o'-woods?" the corporal demanded amiably.

When Good told him, his face serious, Larry laid a hand on the Englishman's knee.

"Listen," he said soberly; "it isn't part of my job to queer another person's deal, but you being a cheechako, I'm going to tell you that Skagway needs a whole lot of watching. And before you decide to buy that claim of his, go to a lawyer and tell him to make sure you get a clear title."

Good nodded, thanked Larry for the hint, and during the rest of the way learnt quite a lot concerning the absent claim-holder's life and methods.

It was three weeks later that, having received word that Skagway had returned from New Westminster, Good loaded his pack and set out for his return visit to the claim. This time he started in the afternoon, instead of, as previously, in the early morning, so that already night had fallen before he reached the fringe of woodland that bordered the clearing in whose centre was Skagway's cabin.

Just as Good was passing into the open, the door opened, and the prospector came out.

On the point of hailing him, suddenly Good checked himself; the next moment had shrunk farther back within cover. It had seemed to him that there was something rather furtive both in the claim-holder's movements, and the way that, before closing the door behind him, he glanced here and there about the clearing, as if to be sure he was not under observation. And, for the love of Mike, Good asked himself, what was a man doing carrying a double-barrelled shot-gun at this time of night?

He watched closely, and coming towards him, Skagway passed into the belt of trees not a dozen yards away; from there, moved off in the direction of the claim.

Instinctively, Good followed; there was plenty of cover, and his moccasins were silent on the thick carpet of leaf mould. When Skagway left

the wood for the smaller clearing where he had
dug his trench, Good remained still within shelter
—watching.

He saw the prospector climb the heap of excavated quartz; give a keen glance to either
hand; then, as if satisfied, raise the gun; fire
into the trench; pass along the top of the quartz
and fire again; reload, and at different points,
empty the second two barrels.

In the same way as he had followed Skagway to
the claim, Good trailed him back to the cabin;
waited within cover until the door had closed.
Then, silently, he loped across the open space
until he was immediately outside the window,
from where a chink between the curtains gave
him a clear view of the room.

Hardmouthed, with narrowed eyes, he watched
Skagway clean the gun and prop it in the corner;
watched him, as well, pick up the three tiny
opaque cylinders that were on the table, and
throw them into the stove.

In these new circumstances, the last thing Good
wanted was that his presence should be known,
so, instead of calling at the cabin, he returned
silently to the wood, made a fire, and supped
frugally from bully beef and biscuits.

Thus, the sun was high the next morning
when, hailing the owner as he crossed the clearing,
Good made his way to the cabin.

The door opened and, unshaven, and in his
stocking feet, Skagway, a red-faced, untended-
looking man with shallow brown eyes and wide
expansive gestures, appeared, beaming welcome.

" Water's a-boilin' an' bacon a-frizzlin'," he
cried, " so come right in an' have some eats.
Then we'll go take a look at the claim."

" I'll be glad to," said Good with sincerity,
and ate a hearty breakfast. After that, and without waiting to clear away, Skagway slipped into
his moccasins, took a prospector's pick and a
shallow tin dish from a shelf, and they set off
through the wood together.

" S'matter of fact," Skagway remarked as the
workings came in sight, " the claim's turnin' out
a sight better even than I'd thought."

" Splendid!" Good responded. " What does
it run?" he went on to ask interestedly.

" We-ll "—Skagway spread his hands—" when
first I started in to dig the trench, I couldn't show
more'n seven or eight dollars to the ton. Pretty
good, even then, I'll tell the world—once you've
got your stamp-mill fixed, it don't cost you
more'n a dollar or two a ton to work, anyway.
But the deeper I went down, the richer colour it
showed. Believe it or not, the last pannin' ran
to fourteen dollars, if a cent."

He turned to the Englishman.

" Shouldn't wonder if there's a pretty rich

seam of highgrade not so far away," he suggested impressively.

Good nodded.

" Begins to look like it," he agreed.

The claim-holder swarmed over the excavated quartz, and dropped into the trench at the point where he had fired his first shot on the night before; detached with his pick a piece of quartz from the face; moved forward, and did so again and, farther on still, a third time.

" That enough?" he demanded, swinging round to Good, who nodded. " Right! Now we'll go pan it," he added purposefully, and when this was done the result was enough fine gold to have quarter-filled a small salt spoon.

" Wadjer think o' *that*?" Skagway cried triumphantly. " Best showin' yet—and taken from all along the trench—not just one place. Must run twenty dollars a ton."

The Englishman nodded slowly.

" Good enough," he agreed. He shot the other a direct glance. " But with as rich a proposition as this, just why are you selling?"

Skagway gave another of his gestures — fatalistic, but resigned.

" It's that old mother of mine," he explained sadly. " She need's me back home; pinin' for me, as you might say. An' as I guess she won't be here for so long, well——"

" I see," Good said, anxious to avoid pathos. And added slowly. " Well, providing you can show a clear title, I'm a buyer at the price."

Skagway laughed shortly on a single note.

" You c'm along to Lawyer Craig's," he said confidently. " He'll show you I've a clear title, all right."

Three days later, in the log-built office of the dry and laconic little Scottish lawyer, the statement proved correct. Skagway had staked the claim himself, put in the necessary work over the necessary period the law demands, paid his dues, and there was the document to prove it.

As Craig was preparing the transfer:

" Ye'll need the signatures witnessing," he pointed out without looking up from his desk.

" Wait," said Good, slipped out of the office and down the street. Here, as he hoped, he met Larry Steer, and told that officer what was required of him.

" What are you paying for that hole in the ground, if it's a fair question?" the corporal demanded, as they made their way down the unmetalled, sun-bathed street.

When Good had told him this:

" Why, man, you're plum crazy—even for a cheechako," Larry protested, and stopped dead in his stride. " Listen," he went on impressively, " it's all right about it being up to every man to look after himself, but you cheechako's aren't fair game—you just haven't a notion of what you're up against. Or *who* you're up against, either, if it comes to a showdown. And when I tell you that Skagway's a snake, that's favourin' him." He glanced comprehensively at the Englishman's clear candid eye. " And *you* ain't no marmozet," he added dryly.

" Maybe not," Good admitted modestly, " but I'm fed to the teeth with doing nothing to earn a living, nevertheless."

Larry snorted scornfully.

" It'll keep you pretty good and busy making a living out of that claim, don't you worry," he said with feeling.

In Craig's office, where by this the transfer was all ready for signature, there was a gleam in Skagway's eyes as he swung round on Good; a less confident gleam as he recognized Larry.

" You got the dough all handy?" he demanded of the former, and the Englishman nodded.

" In bills," he said, produced a wad of currency, counted off the amount; handed it, not to Skagway, but to the lawyer. Who, having counted it, passed a fountain-pen to Skagway.

The document signed, grinning openly, Skagway stuffed the purchase price in his pocket; with one of his wide and expansive gestures, thrust out his hand to the Englishman.

" Now it's all good an' settled—shake!" he cried exuberantly.

Good raised his eyebrows. There was a strained silence.

" With a man who's just unloaded a salted mine on me?" Good said interestedly at last.

If it was not possible for Skagway's leathern-textured face to whiten under the startled glance of the corporal, and the interested one of the Scot, the look in his eyes was revealing.

" You've bought it, ain'tcha?" he shouted. " An' even a cheechako Englishman don't buy no salted mine if he knows it. So—wadyer mean —salted?"

Good reached for the transfer; put it in his pocket.

" I saw you salt it," he said equably. " On the night before, actually, I showed up—four shot-gun barrels of it. Also—through the cabin window—I saw you burn the two quills of placer gold you salted it *with*—and that later I found out you bought from Jimmy Curran."

There was no doubt about it, this reached home, and Skagway showed it; it was a full thirty seconds before he was able to discipline his features.

" And *yet* you bought it!" he sneered.

Good shook his head.

" The salted area is only one small part of the

real claim," he said easily. " It was the area close by—and until I saw what you were after, I intended pointing out to you—in which I happen to be interested."

He produced from his pocket a handful of quartz that, when he tossed it on the table, gleamed faintly in the sunlight that streamed into the room through the uncurtained window.

" Specimens of a rock the rain washed clear of moss on the day I called when you were at New Westminster," he explained, " and that assays just under eight hundred dollars to the ton."

" But "—Larry speaking, trying hard to conceal his astonishment—" how do you come to know highgrade when you see it?"

The Englishman grinned.

" Through the six months' course in geology I took at Manitoba University when I decided to come North," he said.

CHAPTER XIII

Corporal Steer is Surprised

Larry Steer looked up as the orderly room door opened.

"What's your good news, Flying Bird?" he asked easily.

Slightly, but with a queer emphasis, the Ojibway shook his head.

"Bad news," he said dispassionately. "Skookum Charlie killed on the trail."

Larry's breath caught sharply. Skookum Charlie Harriot was one of the best known and popular figures in the Yukon. The corporal found it necessary to keep a firm grip of his voice, as he said:

"How do you mean, killed?"

"Flying Bird find him shot dead," said the Ojibway. "One hour, two hour, after sunrise, as he go to Whitewater Lake for fish."

Larry thrust a couple of days' supplies in his pack, slipped on mackinaw and holster; reached for gauntlets and Stetson.

"Show me," he said curtly.

Whitewater Lake reached, Flying Bird led the

way up a narrow trail through the wood that encroached to the water edge; checked—and pointed.

The body was sprawled across a sudden widening of the trail—a grizzled man, the leathern-textured face hardened to a network of wrinkles; the forehead marred by a dark-rimmed hole.

" Death must have been instantaneous, and there were no signs of a struggle. Larry suspected, indeed, that the actual shooting had taken place elsewhere, for it was his experience that the victim of a bullet falls forward.

" Did you move the body when you found him?" he asked the Ojibway, and there was distaste behind the Indian's headshake.

" Flying Bird not touch um," he said decisively.

So far as Larry could discover, nothing had been stolen either from the dead man's person or from the small hand-toboggan at his side; in the pocket was a wallet containing fifty odd dollars, together with pipe and pouch, cigarettes, match case, small change, hunting knife and magnifying glass.

It was as he made a final dive into one of the trousers pockets that Larry's fingers encountered something small and sharp that proved to be a flake of rock about the size and shape of a ten cent piece, and from which the sunlight that streamed through the foliage overhead struck pinpoints of yellow. It was one of the richest pieces of highgrade quartz he had ever seen.

Puzzled, he thought hard for a moment. After registering a claim, the first thought of a prospector is to send a handful of samples to be assayed.

The presumption, then, was that robbery *was* the motive behind the murder, and to conceal that the dead man had made a strike, the killer had, as he thought, removed all evidence to that effect; it was easy to understand how that tiny piece of quartz had been overlooked. So the odds were a hundred to one that the next man who called in to register a highgrade claim would be the murderer.

Meantime, the Ojibway would know if any strangers had been seen hereabouts, and the old chief, Front Man, was by way of being a friend of his own.

Looking down on the age-and-illness ravaged face of the old man lying on his caribou robe in the dimly lighted tepee, Larry knew that he was looking as well on the passing of one of the last of the old-time Red Men.

He greeted Larry, who had spent many hours seated in the same tent listening to tales of former days, with something that approximated to a smile. Then, after they had exchanged greetings:

" Sorry, Chief, but this time I've called, not for a chat, but for information," Larry said levelly.

The old man nodded.

" Skookum Charlie he die on the trail," he said confirmatively.

" *Shot* on the trail," Larry corrected, " so that the killer could jump his claim. Any strangers around here lately?"

The old chief made a feeble but expressive gesture indicative of his own helplessness.

" How should Front Man know?" he said. " Go into the camp, and there ask those who hunt and fish."

But the more men Larry questioned, the more puzzled he became. Hunting, fishing, and wood-cutting, between them the tribe covered every acre of the surrounding country, and with the exception of Skookum himself, who had called in one evening for a chat with Front Man, not one had seen, or detected, signs of any stranger about the locality.

It was as Larry was passing through the camp on his way out that, at the entrance of a tepee, he caught sight of Bear's Cap, Front Man's six-year-old great-grandchild—a sloe-eyed imp of mischief who was one of the corporal's favourites.

" Hello, youngster," he greeted, pulling up.

" What do you think you're doing? Juggling?"

Gazing solemnly at Larry, the boy gathered up the three stones of which he had been attempting to keep two in the air at once.

" Redcoat try," he suggested, and so eagerly that, in spite of his own preoccupation, Larry laughed.

" Sure," he agreed, arranged two of the pieces in his right hand and a third in his left. Only, as the first of the two rose into the air, and he came to fill the vacancy with the one from his other hand, to stand gazing silently at what that hand received.

" Where did you get this, Bear's Cap?" he asked quietly.

The boy looked at him hard for a moment before, realizing that here was something more momentous than his own undetected sin, he began to cry. So Larry swung the penitent to his shoulder, and strolled off to a spot immediately outside the camp limits.

It cost him a full half-hour, an apple, and a bar of chocolate to gain the boy's confidence, but when it came, confession was full, unrestricted and, to the corporal, to the last degree both surprising and illuminating.

Eventually, he left Bear's Cap at the entrance to his tepee, and passed swiftly to the one occupied by the chief.

His breath coming more faintly now, even than before, Front Man was able to read his visitor's mood.

" You bring bad news," he said in a weak but confident voice.

Slowly, deliberately, his glance on the faded, deeply-set eyes that met his own so purposefully, Larry nodded.

" To myself, at least," he said levelly, " the worst news that I could have heard. Who was the man that, by your orders, shot and killed Skookum Charlie, and "—he opened his hand to display what he had acquired from Bear's Cap—" robbed him of—this?"

The chief's glance dropped to the piece of highgrade in Larry's hand, and upward to his face again.

" Bear's Cap swipe a piece from my tepee— for all my threats," he said, not without pride.

" And the remainder?" Larry demanded.

" Buried," the chief replied with finality.

There was a long silence. Eventually:

" Now, Front Man," Larry said coldly, " you shall tell me who it was that you ordered to shoot Skookum Charlie—and for what reason."

Something of the old arrogance flashed into the face of the dying chief.

" When Front Man wishes that there is shooting, it is Front Man who presses the trigger," he said, his voice as cold as Larry's had been a moment before.

" You mean," Larry demanded, when astonishment permitted him to speak, " that it was *you* who shot Skookum Charlie? In *your* state?"

" As sometimes a dying fire will leap to a last fierce flame, so, sometimes, do they who die," the chief said with a shrug of his emaciated shoulders.

" But *why*, Chief?" Larry cried in distress. " A decent old-timer like Skookum!"

The figure on the caribou-robe shrunk as from a threatened blow.

" Listen," Front Man said. " More moons ago than there are cicadas in the trees, the people of my father's father were granted reservation in the State of Nevada, and there lived peacefully, harming none, for full two score years. But on an evil day a white man found gold on that land, and after that there was no more peace, but only shooting, so that the Ojibway fled."

Larry nodded. He had heard and read much of those years of Indian betrayal across the border.

" Later," the chief went on slowly, " my people were given other land in another place, and again they lived peacefully, harming none. But again a white man found gold, and again, after much shooting, the Ojibway were driven from their homes.

" This time they crossed the border to find sanctuary in Canada, and here for many years have lived in peace. . . . And two days since, a white man came into my tent and showed me gold he had found on the border of our land."

Painfully the dying chief raised himself from the caribou-robe to look deeply into Larry's eyes.

" And because where there is gold, there, also, is evil," he said gravely, " to preserve our land from that evil, and for my people after I have gone, I, Front Man, Chief of the Ojibway, slew him."

CHAPTER XIV

A Question of Time

There was a knock at the door of the orderly-cum-living-room. Larry looked up from the typewriter from which he was laboriously tapping a patrol report.

"What's eating you, Pierre?" he inquired of the squat, dark figure who entered.

The leather-textured, almost circular face of Louis Pierre Lefevre showed darker, even, than customarily; the tiny deep-set eyes beneath the jet-black half-moons of brows snapped vividly with excitement.

"You come wit' me—now?" he cried urgently.

Casually, unemotionally, Larry reached for the short blackened pipe he had discarded in the preoccupation of composition; pressed down the tobacco; relighted it. He had all kinds of use for this little French-Canadian trapper, inclined to excitability though he knew him to be.

"Suppose you stop dancing the Big Apple, or whatever it is, and tell what the trouble is," he said equably.

Arms outflung, the *habitant* made a wide gesture of protest.

" Ah-h, you Englishers!" he cried, scornfully vibrant. " 'Ow, always you think because you all-same iceberg, you must also be the big strong man!" Spatulate hands outspread across the desk, his snapping eyes bored into the lean, salient-jawed face confronting him. " But if you see what, not one hour ago, was revealed to Pierre Lefevre, maybe even you, the great police-officer, would lose some small *aplomb*. For, I tell you, it is a sight that is not ver' pretty."

Larry knew that in a crisis there was no one more reliable than his visitor, so that an event that had power to work the little man to his present pitch was something out of the ordinary.

" Maybe in your own good time you'll spill whatever it is that's biting you," he said encouragingly.

" No!" The negative was emphatic. " For, because I think it better you see for yourself, I spill not'ing. You come with Louis Pierre."

Slowly Larry levered his rawboned frame to the upright, unhurriedly gathered his papers together, placed them in a folder, and the folder in a drawer; buckled on belt and holster; reached for his Stetson.

" How far?" he said, and caught the other's quick sigh of relief.

" One hour," the *habitant* replied. " If you no' go to sleep on the way, that is. An' if you do, I report you." He cocked a bright eye. " And for the *habitant*, Louis Pierre Lefevre, to put up a complaint about *le très magnifique* Corporal Steer, would be all-same your pride suffer a swift kick in those so-lovely yellow striped pants of which, doubtless, you are so proud."

" The last complaint registered against me— by Charlie McNutt it was, if mem'ry serves— the Old Man said the next that came along he'd have me court-martialled and broke. . . . Or was that the complaint before the last? One of 'em, anyway," Larry said reflectively, when they were outside.

The *habitant's* shoulders and eyebrows travelled upward.

" An' three weeks later the great McNutt was sent for two years to the woodpile for 'ighgradin'," he remarked, beady eyes expressionlessly on the trail ahead. A moment, however, and he shifted his glance inquiringly to Larry. " An' Slim Bellerby, he report you also?" he asked.

Larry nodded.

" For neglect of duty, in that, whilst on patrol, I spent a week fishing Elbow Creek with Bear's Fang, from the Ojibway Reserve," he confirmed gravely.

Louis Pierre ejected tobacco juice.

" And less than one month after that, you bring in Slim for peddlin' hooch to the Indians, so that he go for one year to the cooler also," he observed.

The lank corporal's shoulders twitched reminiscently—an Indian tepee contains more inhabitants than human ones, and the seven days he had occupied in gaining the confidence of the young chief on the subject of illicit liquor had been more successful than hygienic. Still, that was how it went, and that greasy bootlegger had been a thorn in his side longer than Larry cared to think about.

" Some'ow," Louis Pierre said reflectively, " I think there are quite a lot around these parts 'oo would throw up their 'ats if they 'ear you were leavin' for the Outside. . . . And if there is another in the 'ole Territory 'oo could 'ave made that wooden Indian talk, Louis Pierre not know of 'im."

Larry knocked out his pipe; ground the dottle hard and carefully beneath his heel. Smouldering tobacco shares with unextinguished camp-fires the responsibility for nine forest fires in ten, and here the trail passed through a wood, with the dead leaves and pine needles tinder-dry underfoot. The gloom of olive-dark foliage relieved startlingly by the high colouring of moosemaple and dogwood, the Hunting Wind of Autumn stirred the branches overhead; from either side of the trail

7

came the rustlings of tiny furred creatures foraging for winter supplies. Of all the year, it was the time Larry loved best.

When at last they passed to open ground, the harebell-blue backing of the distant hills was checkered harlequin-fashion by the vivid scarlet of maple and, at their foot, the dark saffron of sedgegrass. Inhaling deeply of air aromatic with sage and cherry leaves:

" The Four Way Lodge is open, all right," Larry commented, using the Indian term for the hunting season.

Tiny eyes sombre, wide-lipped mouth hard, the *habitant* nodded.

" It's to be prayed *le bon Dieu* will not permit repeated the first shoot of the season," he said soberly.

Because he was able to read behind that repression a seething excitement, and, oddly, a deep resentment, Larry schooled his voice.

" That sounds pretty grim," he said indifferently, and the *habitant* snorted rather than spoke his reply.

" Grim enough," he said, " to bring the little bow-legged man from Ottawa."

Then it was that Larry knew what it was he was being called upon to investigate. Two years before, when there had been a bad killing in Dawson, the executioner dispatched from Ottawa had fitted in every way with the French-Canadian's description.

" What's Fenoughty been up to?" he demanded, for, apart from the one on Good's claim, and that lay well to the west, the cabin of that unpleasantly-tempered Irishman was the only one within a two-days' patrol; one that he, personally, visited only as often as his duty required.

Before the *habitant* could reply, rounding a turn in the trail ahead, a tall lithe figure approached them with the long gliding step of those who are accustomed more to snowshoes than moccasins.

" What is Questing Wolf doin' in this neck-of-the-woods?" the *habitant* questioned suspiciously.

" Why shouldn't he be here?" the corporal demanded practically, for, choosing the free life of the trail rather than what he regarded as Government wet-nursing, the young Ojibway had cut adrift from Reservation. " You don't suspect him of having anything to do with— whatever it is you're dragging me to see?"

Louis Pierre's headshake was emphatic.

" No, no!" he said. " For at the only time that matters, Questing Wolf was in Tamrack—where 'e come into Barney Hamilton's store for tobacco —an' when 'e 'ad got it, lay in 'is blankets outside all the night t'rough. What I want to know is, what 'e do 'ere *now*?"

"Better ask him," Larry suggested indifferently. Except that in pursuit of his ruling passion he was inclined to hunt game out of season, there was nothing wrong with Questing Wolf that he knew of.

Louis Pierre blocking the trail, the young Ojibway halted. Poker-faced, blank-eyed, he was carrying the small home-made bow that the Northern Indian uses in default of firearms for hunting. From his belt dangled a brace and a half of partridges.

"You 'it the trail pretty good an' early this mornin', I guess," the French-Canadian said, not too cordially.

Dark, high cheek-boned face without warmth or interest, there was nothing furtive in the Ojibway's reaction to the challenge.

"Questing Wolf hunt," he said, and pointed to the partridges. "Trade um for tobacco."

"Pretty fat, these," Larry remarked amiably, his fingers closing about one of the birds. As he wiped his hands on his handkerchief, at the far back of his mind was the genesis of a sudden thought, that for the moment refused to germinate.

"Seen anything of the Fenoughtys?" Louis Pierre demanded quickly and unexpectedly, and the reply came immediately.

"Questing Wolf see no man—red *or* white,"

the Ojibway said calmly, and passed on his way.

As, with the wood behind them, they crossed the scrub towards the Fenoughty cabin, Larry saw that no smoke feathered from the chimney, and that about the lonely log-built shack brooded an indefinable air of desolation.

Louis Pierre was the first to reach the door. And as, his fingers about the handle, he turned to Larry, the circular coarse-grained face was hard.

" I tell you, my frien', it is not pretty, what you will see," he said warningly, and Larry shrugged his shoulders.

" I didn't think you were bringing me to a mannequin parade," he replied practically.

Yet, hard-boiled as ten years service had made him, he found it necessary to take a very firm grip on himself at what that open door disclosed.

The living-room was of the usual rough and uncompromising utility; stove, table and chairs home-made; two spruce-and-chicken-wire bunks covered with green two-point Hudson Bay blankets; caribou skins on the floor.

Forehead to ground, in a semi-kneeling position, crouched the body of a middle-aged man, the floor at the point of contact telling horribly of how he had died.

Face downward at the other end of the room sprawled a second and younger figure.

Lank face expressionless, keen veiled eyes

travelling from one to the other of those victims, absorbing in detail the general effect of the room, and its disposition; searching, more especially, for weapons, Larry stood for a long time motionless without speaking.

At last he crossed to the body of the older man, studied it for a long moment before he turned it face upward. With its two days stubble of beard, thin lips down-drawn to a sneer, the face that stared into his own was immutably savage. There was a small purple-rimmed hole in the wide strip of forehead, with a larger and less regular cavity at the point of exit at the back.

" Been dead for some time, I reckon," Larry remarked at last.

The *habitant*, who had not stirred from his position by the door, nodded.

" Since midnight, or soon after," he said briefly, and Larry studied him speculatively.

" How do you come to know that?" he demanded shortly.

" I tell you—when you've 'ad your look-see," the *habitant* replied levelly.

Knowing his man, Larry knew, also, that, informing and possessing him was some emotion that could not altogether be covered by natural horror of tragedy.

Without speaking, Larry went over to the other figure, to find that while he, too, had been shot through the forehead, here there was a marked difference from that other victim. For where in the case of the father the countenance was of elemental strength, that of the son spoke only of a weakness that was in no way mitigated by the obstinacy of the overhanging brow, and the set of the full, over-sensitive lips.

Larry's own mouth was grim as he pointed, not to the head of the dead man, but to the breast of the crumpled khaki shirt in which, also, was a bullet-hole.

" Looks as if the killer was all set for making a clean job of it," he said laconically.

The *habitant* stepped forward; stood staring unblinkingly at the sprawled, still figure.

" You think 'e die from the one shot, anyway?" he questioned rather breathlessly at length.

Larry swung round on him.

" Only a doctor'll be able to say for sure," he said. His eyes narrowed. " Why didn't you tell me—so's I could've phoned for him to come right along with us?"

" I phoned Liversedge myself," the French-Canadian said curtly. " The old butcher set out from Five Fingers same time as we start from Tamrack, so that 'e should be 'ere now at any minute."

Larry thought over this for a little, and did not like the result. If law and order were to survive, murder was one of those things it was necessary to investigate to formula.

"Listen, you!" he said uncivilly. " If you think you're going to start an unofficial police of your own, you're heading for trouble. The only policemen in this district are myself and Constable Wood. So now you shall tell me how—and all— you come to know of these killings."

In the pause that followed, Larry gained the impression that Louis Pierre was arranging his thoughts into sequence.

" You know the young Englisher 'oo work for Monsieur Good?" he said at last.

Larry's nod was a shade impatient.

" It's my job to know everyone in my district," he replied shortly.

The *habitant's* eyes, fixed intently upon his, were sombre.

" I think, maybe," he said slowly, " it best you shall know, right now, what the Englisher tell me; that 'e was out of camp from ten hour last night, until two hours this mornin'.

" An' when you ask me where was 'e between those times, I 'ave to tell you that 'e come 'ere— to this cabin. For so 'e say when 'e come into Tamrack to tell me, also, that 'e it was 'oo find " —the broad stub-fingered hand gestured to the floor—" *those!*"

Even to the normally shock-proof corporal, this

was pretty startling. Though from his reading of the Englishman, not a bit of the killer type, he would have said, you never knew. And with those wild currents and cross-currents that had come into the young Englishman's life since his arrival in the North. . . .

" Listen," Larry said purposefully, " let's get down to it. What you're trying to tell me, but without a whole lot of love for the job, is that young Callender is the murderer of these two here?"

Moccasined feet dithering on the boards, black eyes blazing, the *habitant* shook clenched fists above his head.

" But no!" he cried. " The Englisher is no killer; I, Louis Pierre Lefevre, swear it. 'E still wet behind the ears, but 'e good feller. . . . 'E nearly go crazy when 'e arrive 'ere to find, instead of that old moron Fenoughty an' 'is boy, only two dead men."

" Why didn't he report it to me?" Larry asked shortly.

Slowly the *habitant*'s spatulate hands descended to thrump dejectedly against his thighs.

" But that is what for 'e come into Tamrack," he protested.

" I don't remember seeing him," Larry pointed out dryly.

" Ah!" Palpably Louis Pierre was striving to

7*

bring conviction. " You know what these chee-chakos from the Old Country are? Timid—not for themselves, but of the North and its customs. So, when Callender reach town, and 'e begin to think what like is the steel cage in the barracks, and how 'e will 'ave to spend month after month in the pen at Dawson before the trial—'is 'eart, I say, went yellow, and in 'is fear 'e come to the one friend 'e 'ave in the North—to me, Louis Pierre—to ask what shall 'e do?"

There were steps outside. The door swung open and Doctor Liversedge came in, huge, red-faced and corpulent; with him a boy of twenty-five or so, tall and slim and fair-haired, the texture of whose now whitened face remained as yet uncoarsened by the moistureless air of the North; whose eyes, resting for a fractional moment on the floor, turned to glance feverishly at the uninformative face of the constable. Also a small, dark-eyed boy two or three years younger.

The *habitant*, his round face working, took a quick step towards them, but, as if deciding that it was better to await events, only to check himself. After a quick glance at the newcomers, Larry turned directly to the doctor.

" Two dead," he said, and pointed.

There was a certain triumph on the surgeon's coarse-featured face that, to Larry, failed entirely to appeal. Actually, Dr. Liversedge disliked

Larry and the *habitant* only a little less than he disliked Englishmen in general.

" You're telling me!" he exclaimed. " No need for any Sherlock Holmes stuff here; I've brought the killer along with me—*and* his accomplice. All you've got to do is put the irons on him and run him into the cooler."

Only for a moment the corporal allowed his glance to rest on the suspects before turning his eyes to the sprawled figures on the floor.

The elder boy spoke, his voice firmer than Larry would have anticipated from his appearance.

" I'm no more responsible for these deaths, Corporal," he said, " than you are."

" Splendid!" Larry said easily. " In a minute or two you shall say all you have in your mind." He turned directly to Doctor Liversedge. " Meanwhile, you might do your stuff, Doc."

On his knees before the elder victim, the doctor looked up disparagingly.

" Shot through the brain, of course," he said. " When'll the Superintendent be here from Dawson?"

" When I send for him, I shouldn't wonder," Larry replied.

Wide face darkened, the doctor's heavy body swung back on to his heels.

" You know it's the rule that all cases of major

crime have to be reported immediately to Division," he said aggressively. " So's officers can be sent who know the job."

Larry, however, refused to rise to the bait.

" It's you who're telling *me*, this time," he said amiably. " And just the minute I'm convinced that a major crime's been committed, I'll put the call through—if I feel like it."

Scowling, the surgeon raised himself laboriously to his feet, strode over to what once had been the younger Fenoughty. Here again his examination of the head wound was only cursory. Nor did he linger when, unencumbered by the coarse canvas shirt, the chest wound was exposed.

" One bullet through the brain," he said; " the other in the chest."

Larry nodded.

" Even my defective intelligence was able to gather that," he said easily. " Would the one in the chest be fatal, do you think—independent of the head wound?"

The surgeon did not hesitate.

" Surest thing you know," he said, his voice truculent. " Any weapons found?"

For a moment, however, Larry allowed the question to pass unanswered.

" Instantaneous? It's still the chest wound I'm asking about," he pressed, and this time there was the slightest pause before the reply.

" Sure it'd be instantaneous," the surgeon said definitely at last.

Larry seemed to consider this for a moment.

" I'll have the bodies sent into Tamrack for the inquest right away," he said at last.

" And take the killer with you?" the doctor said curtly.

Before, however, Larry could speak, the French-Canadian broke in. He had been keeping a very firm grip on himself hitherto, but now, quivering with excitement, he exploded.

" Killer, *nothing*!" he cried, and pointed a vibrant forefinger at Callender who, his hand protectively about his companion's arm, was leaning against the wall. " Can you think that boy a killer?"

" I can think of anyone as a killer—given a strong enough motive," Larry said soberly, and now his eyes, narrowed and speculative, were undeviatingly upon the Englishman, who did not flinch under the scrutiny.

Callender, his pale face flushed, but eyes more resolute than they had been, was on the point of speaking, but the younger boy forestalled him.

" Tommy here's no more a killer than you are yourself," he said, his protest levelled, not at Larry, but at the doctor. " As he'll tell you himself, he's in a jam, all right, no getting away from that." Larry observed how persistently he kept his eyes from those grim aftermaths of tragedy on the floor. " But he never laid a hand on the Fenoughtys."

The doctor's voice broke in.

" It wasn't a hand that's caused the trouble," he said harshly. " It was bullets—that don't have to get to close quarters."

Larry let this pass; he turned to the boy.

" What are you doing here, anyway?" he asked quietly.

To his satisfaction it was Callender who replied. Though his hand was clasped so tightly about his companion's arm that Larry wondered he did not wince with the pain of it, he had himself in hand.

" Louis Pierre advised us to come," he said. " To explain to you. We caught up with Doctor Liversedge on the way."

Larry nodded.

" And explained to him?" he questioned.

Callender's colour deepened.

" He had to know sooner or later, anyway— and I'd been nursing it all the morning," he muttered.

" Nursing what?" Larry asked.

" That I was here in the middle of the night, and found "—he gestured dumbly to the floor— " *those*."

The doctor sneered audibly.

" You mean, that's how you *left* 'em!" he broke in antagonistically.

" What *made* you come here in the middle of the night?" Larry inquired of Callender without comment, and watched the quick look that passed between the two.

" To tell Dan Fenoughty to leave off pestering Jimmy Forbes, here," Callender said hotly. " He'd told him that—that——"

He hesitated, and the other took him up.

" That I'd pay him what I owed soon's I drew my wages at the end of the season," he said resolutely.

" Why not tell him yourself?" Larry demanded, and watched the hot colour flood into his face.

" Tell him! I told him so often I got to say it by heart," he almost shouted.

" What was it you owed him money for?" Larry demanded.

" Cards," the boy replied. " Dan used to sneak out to my camp after his father had gone to bed—and I lost all the time. When I said I couldn't pay, he said it didn't matter; it could wait until I drew my wages at the end of the season. I lost so persistently that I got the idea he wasn't playing straight. When I told him I was through playing for good, he started pressing me for back reckonings; threatened to tell Mr. Good if I didn't come through——"

It was Louis Pierre who broke into the pause that followed. He looked directly across at Larry.

"Always Dannie was just chore-boy to old man Fenoughty," he explained. "And as well as the black Irisher was jealous of anyone Dannie kind of liked, 'e wasn't 'aving 'is unpaid servant away from 'is work; 'e wanted 'im there all the time. So, when he know Dannie 'as a date with Jimmy Forbes or anyone else, 'e would set the boy on chores to keep 'im at 'ome."

The doctor sniffed derisively.

"Maybe that import from London, England, who was working for Good as well, wasn't above standing in at those card games," he said unpleasantly.

Forbes, however, was not having this.

"I'd quit playing and sent Dannie out on his ear before ever Callender showed up," he protested. "The trouble was, Dannie wouldn't take no for an answer. Yesterday afternoon, while Mr. Good was on the claim, he came around crying out that if he wasn't paid, he was going to ask my boss for the money right away."

Poker faced, Larry nodded.

"Callender's a great friend of yours, isn't he?" he asked.

Forbes, in turn, nodded.

" Just lately, anyway," he agreed. " At first
I was just kind of sorry for him—so far from his
own folk, and bein' so strange to our ways.
Then, as I got to know him better, I liked him
fine." He hesitated. " It got so that, instead of
me looking after him it was the other way around
—I started in to rely on him."

" Did he know about those poker games with
Fenoughty?" Larry asked.

Forbes looked doubtful.

" If he didn't actually know, I guess he'd a
mighty good idea," he replied, with an uneasy
glance at the Englishman.

" And when he called last night, you told him
all about it?" Larry suggested. " The way young
Fenoughty was dunning and threatening you?"

It was Callender who replied, and with considerable force.

" Just as I was going," he admitted. " Even
then I had to drag it out of him." His face
darkened. " And I made up my mind it had to
stop. Once and for all."

Doctor Liversedge's laugh was unpleasant.

" You saw it stopped, all right," he agreed
significantly, and still Larry ignored him. Louis
Pierre, however, did not. Eyes blazing, he took
a step forward.

" You keep that trap of yours shut," he said,
his own mouth tight-lipped. " You are 'ere, not

to throw dirt at the Englisher, but only to say just 'ow—and when—these men die. And that is going to take all your time, for only if your brain was as good as your voice is loud, would you be as clever as you think."

Liversedge cried, furiously:

" I don't need any butting in from you, any-way."

" If you two've finished your cross-talk," Larry said equably, " I'll get on with my questioning. " And if you don't want me to clear the court, you'll keep quiet—both of you. Being only an untutored corporal of police, if I need any help, I'll not be too proud to ask for it."

He turned once more to Callender.

" And having made up your mind Dan had to quit his threatening," he inquired, " how did you set about making sure he did?"

Haggard-eyed, the Englishman braced himself.

" As I was due on the claim at six this morn-ing," he said, his voice not quite steady, " I came here straight away—so I'd be sure of finding Dannie at home."

His hands clasped and unclasped nervously.

" What time did you reach here?" Larry asked quietly.

" I looked at my watch when I was a mile or so away, and it was a quarter to twelve," Cal-lender replied without hesitation.

" And then?" Larry pressed, breaking into the silence.

Callender braced his shoulders. Highly strung as, undoubtedly, he was, he was not without courage, it occurred to Larry.

" What surprised me was to find the shack lighted," he said slowly. " Dan was always complaining to Jimmy that the old man was so mean with his coal-oil he made a practice of hitting the hay soon after sundown, and made Dan do the same. I was more surprised still when I knocked at the door and there was no reply I listened, and no sound came from inside."

Horror showed in his face as he hesitated. " Don't know if you'll believe me," he said, more slowly still, " but there was something about the silence I felt was kind of un-natural. . . ."

" It's not what you felt, but what you did— and saw—I'm interested in," Larry reminded.

" After a little, I tried the door," Callender responded hoarsely. " It wasn't locked; I wish it had been. I went in. . . . Inside, Dan and old man Fenoughty were—as they are now."

As if in relief, he used his free hand and a large silk handkerchief to wipe his forehead.

" And you did—what?" Larry demanded.

The reply came reluctantly, but with candour.

"Panicked! The shock and the appalling unexpectedness of it. . . . And they looked so—awful. . . . And the silence. . . . I just rushed out of the shack—and to my own camp —to think out what to do. . . . Then, as soon as it was light, I went to Jimmy, and told him what had happened. He suggested I put the position before Louis Pierre. Louis Pierre said to do nothing until he'd been here to see for himself. And he came straight away."

Larry looked inquiringly at the *habitant*—who shrugged shoulders that were disproportionately broad for his height.

"I do what I think best," he said levelly. "If what the Englisher says is true, then no 'arm could come in seeing for myself—the two were dead, anyway. When I find that what 'e tell me *is* true, I go back and say for 'im to come 'ere, where you will be waiting. . . . Then I come and fetch you."

Possessed as Louis Pierre was with the typical Frenchman's logic of mind, Larry was prepared to accept this. He turned to Callender.

"During the time you were here last night, did you see any pistol lying around?" he inquired, and the answer came immediately.

"Sure. A Colt .45 Service pattern revolver. But you'll already be taking care of that, I expect."

" Whereabouts was it?" Larry asked, and watched Callender's eyes turn towards the younger of those shrouded figures.

" On the floor. Six feet or so to the right of Dan," he said confidently.

" Says you!" This from the doctor, his wide face set in a sneer. " Maybe you'd like to tell us where it is right now?"

For the first time in that strained interview Larry showed signs of temper. Lean jaw salient, and wide mouth hard.

" When I want any comment from you," he said, " I'll ask for it. Meantime, anything more like that, and, police doctor or not, you'll be out of this shack on your ear and at the rate of knots."

Face enpurpled, untended body quivering:

" Just the minute I get back to Five Fingers, I'll 'phone a report about you to division," the surgeon shouted.

" But before that," Larry said, " you'll make a post-mortem on Dan Fenoughty."

For one long, antagonistic moment, the other regarded him searchingly.

" Are you trying to teach me my business?" he said unpleasantly at last.

" So far as such a heart-breaking task's possible," Larry conceded. " Meantime, I'm having that post-mortem. I'm not arguing, I'm telling you."

There was in his voice a confidence it was not expedient for the doctor to override. Before he could reply, moreover, Larry was speaking again.

"Another thing. About that adverse report there's all the talk about. Send it in if you like —it'll only add to the Old Man's collection, anyway. But if you don't want to figure as to-day's big laugh, you'll wait until after the P.M.—and then not send it." He turned to the *habitant*. "Help me carry Dan into Tamrack. The old man can wait until later."

As they were improvising a stretcher from the blankets:

"What are you doing with me?" the English boy demanded, for in the last few minutes the policeman had paid him no attention.

Larry glanced at his own finger-tips.

"Go find that old perisher, Questing Wolf, and bring him into barracks," he instructed. "If he raises any kind of kick, tell him I'll fetch him in myself—in irons."

"You're crazy, man!" The doctor again, his voice derisive. "Didn't you hear Louis Pierre say the In'jun spent the night outside the store? And the Fenoughtys've been dead twelve to sixteen hours."

"I shouldn't wonder a bit," Larry conceded amicably. "But it's not who was he with last night, but how he spent this morning, I'm interested in. Go find him, Callender."

The small procession trudged the miles in silence; while Larry and the *habitant's* attention was devoted to negotiating their grim burden over the root- and rock-strewn trail, the doctor, whose not infrequent clashes with the lank and uncommunicative corporal had taught him a considerable, if grudging, respect for that blazer of trails, was seething, but cautious.

Unobtrusively, they took the body to the lean-to shed at the back of the Happy Trapper saloon, that was the local substitute for a mortuary. While the doctor went to his own shack for food, Larry took the *habitant* to the barracks for a meal.

"Now you shall get busy," he said, when, suspicious, but commendably prompt to time, Liversedge appeared.

"Get busy with *what?*" the doctor snapped.

"Finding out which of those two shot-wounds came first," Sourdough replied.

"What's it matter, anyway?" the surgeon demanded explosively.

"I'll tell you," Larry's manner was authoritative. "If Dan Fenoughty was shot through the head *before* he was shot through the chest—which I'll bet a month's pay and allowances he wasn't—then I'll go hunt the murderer. But if the chest-wound came first, the case is open-and-shut."

There was the sound of moccasined feet on the veranda outside; following a knock, the door opened. Callender and Forbes; with them, poker-faced, Questing Wolf, the Ojibway.

Lithe and upright, he stood immediately facing the table where the corporal was seated. To the others it seemed an interminable time wherein the eyes of the two men held, until at last Larry's voice broke into the silence.

" Remember that partridge of yours I was looking at on the trail this morning?" he said conversationally.

The Indian's high cheek-boned face remained expressionless as, without speaking, he nodded.

" A pretty powerful bow, that'd send an arrow clean through a bird of that size—so that anyone handling it gets blood on their finger-tips and on their palm?" Larry suggested.

There was the faintest flicker in the expressionless eyes of the Ojibway.

" Questing Wolf fire shot," he said.

" With a bow and arrow—as *well* as with a revolver?" Larry questioned easily.

Leisurely, he got up from his chair, went round the table, and to the back of the Indian. His hands went to a bulging hip-pocket; came away holding a heavy-calibre revolver.

For the first time the Ojibway's glance fell; there was the uneasy slur of moccasined feet on the floor. Larry's face was iron hard as he said:

" Anything to say against me arresting you on the charge of murdering Mike and Dan Fenoughty?"

The doctor took a step forward.

" You're crazy, man! Don't you know that Injun was——" he began excitedly, but Larry's hand—and what he was able to read in those narrowed eyes—checked him.

" That'll be all from you," Larry said purposefully, and groped in the desk drawer, produced a pair of handcuffs.

Perceptibly, the Ojibway shrank back.

" Questing Wolf no kill Fenoughty," he stated swiftly.

Larry examined the weapon; turned from it to a book he took from the same drawer as had produced the handcuffs. His thumb turned the book's counterfoils; settled on one.

" This is the gun I issued a permit to Mike Fenoughty for," he said. " How come that Fenoughty is dead—and that you are carrying it?"

There was another silence, wherein the Ojibway's eyes were upon anything but the lean face of the corporal. Then he shrugged narrow shoulders.

" Gun no use to dead man, anyway," he said with the indifference to tragedy of his race. " Questing Wolf shoot two birds—with arrows. Then he go to trade birds with Fen'ty for hooch. But when he reach the cabin, both Fen'tys are dead—and on the floor is a gun. Gun no use to dead men—but heap use to Questing Wolf. On the way home, Questing Wolf shoot another bird—with gun."

Contemplatively, Larry " broke " the weapon; examined the cylinders. Three cartridges remained of the seven that it had held originally.

" How many shots did you fire—altogether?" he questioned.

The Ojibway's lips curled.

" Questing Wolf see that with one shot fired, one bird fall," he said definitely.

" If I did my duty, I'd put you in the pen on a charge of theft and carrying concealed firearms," Larry said, with a glance at the doctor. " Only, as I'm always being told duty's the last thing to worry me—beat it!"

Without comment, resentment, or gratitude, the Ojibway left.

" Those Injuns," Louis Pierre observed, " would trade their mother and all their ancestors for anything that fires a bullet."

Larry got to his feet.

" We'll get across for the post-mortem," he said.

The doctor was thoughtful as they made their way down the straggling, unmetalled street. Even now, he suspected, all the imperturbable corporal's cards were not on the table.

Inside the makeshift mortuary, with Forbes and the Englishman awaiting them outside, Larry locked the door behind them. Then, purposefully, he turned to the doctor.

" Are you absolutely certain," he inquired, " that death from that chest wound would be instantaneous?"

The reply came only after an infinitesimal pause.

" I've said so once, haven't I?" Liversedge replied aggressively at last.

Slowly, thoughtfully, Larry nodded.

" In that case, of course," he said interrogatively, " there'll be no evidence of internal bleeding?"

" There's no hæmorrhage after death, if that's what you're trying to get at," the doctor confirmed impatiently.

" Then, when you come to make the autopsy," Larry pressed, " if you find evidence of bleeding, in itself that will be proof Fenoughty lived for some little time after the wound was inflicted?"

In this cross-examination the expression on the doctor's wide red face had grown cumulatively less confident. Now he shrugged dubiously.

" *If* I find hæmorrhage," he conceded reluctantly.

Larry pointed to the bag of instruments on the floor.

" Then get busy," he said shortly, and there was an interval.

Eventually, as Liversedge stepped back from his unpleasant work, his self-confidence was not so much in evidence as usual.

" You're dead right," he muttered grudgingly. " The whole chest's flooded. Fenoughty must have lived quite a few minutes after that first shot."

Larry might have been heard to expel long withheld breath.

" Now I guess I'll show *you* something," he said.

He leant over the dead man; with his penknife carefully scraped the dried blood from about the bullet-hole in the forehead. Then he turned questioningly to Liversedge—who nodded reluctantly.

" Scorched," he admitted, " from powder."

" Then," Larry said comfortably, " I guess we can pack up. Except for the inquest, the case is closed."

" *Whoops!*" shouted Louis Pierre; wide face

beaming and tiny eyes glinting; strode to the door; threw it open. Forbes's hand clasped tightly about Callender's arm, the pair were standing in a corner of the hotel veranda. They started to their feet as the *habitant* appeared.

"You can beat it off 'ome," he cried exultantly.

Motionless, they looked at him in silence.

"You mean the corporal doesn't suspect me any more?" Callender cried at last.

Louis Pierre hastened to reassure him.

"I do not think he ever did suspect you," he said. "What 'appened is that though Dannie is too scared of the old man to put up any kind of kick, always 'e kick against the way 'e is treated —all-same 'e is a baby. After what the old man say when 'e come 'ome after seeing Forbes, something inside Dannie—breaks, as, if 'e is pushed 'ard enough, will come to the weakest— so that 'e not afraid any more. . . . With Dannie making a stand for maybe the first time in 'is life, the old man pull a gun—just to scare 'im, I guess—and with Dannie as 'e was then, that was not wise.

"Dannie snatch at the gun—an' before 'e know, 'e shoots, an' old man Fenoughty fall dead. Then Dannie, 'oo by now I think is mad in more ways than one, turn the gun on 'imself —to the 'eart. But 'e—not very good shot. . . .

So—'e 'ave to try again—this time to the 'ead."

He glanced inquiringly at Larry over his shoulder.

" I guess that right?" he demanded.

Larry, in turn, glanced inquiringly at Liversedge—who nodded.

" I guess so," the doctor agreed reluctantly.